Camelot

Camelot

edited by Jane Yolen

illustrated by Winslow Pels

Philomel Books   New York

Compilation copyright © 1995 by Jane Yolen
Illustrations copyright © 1995 by Winslow Pels
All rights reserved. This book, or parts thereof, may not be reproduced
in any form without permission in writing from the publisher.
Philomel Books, a division of The Putnam & Grosset Group,
200 Madison Avenue, New York, NY 10016. Published simultaneously in Canada.
Philomel Books, Reg. U.S. Pat. & Tm. Off.
''The Changing of the Shrew'' © 1995 by Kathleen Kudlinski.
''Wild Man'' © 1995 by Diana L. Paxson.
''Once and Future'' © 1995 by Terry Pratchett.
''Gwenhwyfar'' © 1995 by Lynne Pledger.
''Excalibur'' © 1995 by Anne E. Crompton.
''Black Horses for a King'' © 1995 by Anne McCaffrey.
''Holly and Ivy'' © 1995 by James D. Macdonald and Debra Doyle.
''The Raven'' © 1995 by Nancy Springer.
''All the Iron of Heaven'' © 1995 by Mark W. Tiedemann.
''The Amesbury Song'' © 1995 by Jane Yolen and Adam Stemple.
''Our Hour of Need'' © 1995 by Greg Costikyan.
Printed in the United States
Book design by Patrick Collins
The text is set in Garamond #3.

Library of Congress Cataloging-in-Publication Data
Camelot / edited by Jane Yolen; illustrated by Winslow Pels. p. cm.
Summary: A collection of ten short stories and one song exploring the comic, tragic,
and magical adventures of King Arthur, Merlin, and the other inhabitants of Camelot.
1. Arthurian romances. 2. Short stories, American. [1. Arthur,
King—Fiction. 2. Short stories.] I. Yolen, Jane. II. Pels, Winslow, ill.
PZ5.C168 1995 [Fic]—dc20 92-39322 CIP AC ISBN 0-399-22540-4

3 5 7 9 10 8 6 4 2

Contents

Welcome to Camelot by Jane Yolen   1

The Changing of the Shrew Kathleen Kudlinski   5

Wild Man Diana L. Paxson   17

Once and Future Terry Pratchett   41

Gwenhwyfar Lynne Pledger   63

Excalibur Anne E. Crompton   79

Black Horses for a King Anne McCaffrey   93

Holly and Ivy James D. Macdonald and
      Debra Doyle   125

The Raven Nancy Springer   137

All the Iron of Heaven Mark W. Tiedemann   153

Amesbury Song Jane Yolen and Adam Stemple   176

Our Hour of Need Greg Costikyan   181

Illustrations

facing page

Humming a perfect A-flat, he stepped out   6
   through the window and drifted toward the
   kitchens below.

The young men who were chosen for the role   22
   seemed to lose their human manners . . .

I was trying to make penicillin.   54

"They'll be leaving again at daybreak for Camelot,   70
   and you will be leaving with them . . ."

In her arms the Lady carries a long, slender   86
   package wrapped in brown wool.

He had me dangling from the end of his lead   118
   chain like a rat in a bullterrier's jaws.

Lancelot, the buttertub still in one hand, vaulted   134
    into the saddle and galloped from the hall.

Even now that hundreds of years have come and   150
    gone he is not forgotten.

Gadis lifted body after body, part after part, and   166
    helped carry the scattered fragments of combat
    to the pyres.

"Then I will stay," Jose said, "to cover your   182
    retreat."

Welcome to Camelot

When I was eight years old I first entered the doors of Camelot. The story was spelled out on the pages of a very odd encyclopedia my parents had given me called *The Book of Knowledge*. The encyclopedia was not organized in the usual alphabetical way but was instead put together in great clumps of wonderful tales. One of the first sections I encountered was the one about the world of King Arthur.

Once I discovered Arthur, I read about him over and over and over again, sounding out the wonderful names: Merlin, Guinevere, Lancelot, Mordred, Morgain Le Fey—and probably getting all the pronunciations dead wrong. The great deeds—glorious, treacherous, murderous, marvelous—became imprinted upon my heart. I played at King Arthur for months, forcing my younger brother Steven and my best friend, Diane Sheffield, to play the wicked roles while I was, in turn, Arthur, Lancelot, and Merlin.

It was a year later that I discovered Howard Pyle's *The Story of King Arthur and His Knights,* and the year after that T. H. White's *The Sword in the Stone,* and by then I was terribly, wonderfully, finally hooked.

In college I studied Arthurian literature, reading all the required texts. I learned that the historical Arthur—as opposed to the legendary Arthur—was probably not a king at all but rather a heroic British cavalry general named Arthurius. I learned that knights of the day would not have been wearing shining armor but rather leather or chain mail with possibly some leftover Roman-style legionary stuff. And, as one of my professors explained, horses would have been a very late introduction from the Continent—if they were introduced at all. At any rate, Arthur and his knights were probably not very good riders and their horses not very handsome steeds. The authors of the Arthurian stories we know the best wrote centuries after the times of Arthur and used their own ideas of dress and horsemanship.

Did that spoil things for me? Not a bit. If Arthur never really was—well, I believed he still always would be. At least he *would be* in my mind and heart. And he *would be* in the stories I continued to read and enjoy, like Mary Stewart's Arthurian trilogy, Marion Zimmer Bradley's *The Mists of Avalon,* Parke Godwin's books, and Nikolai Tolstoy's books, and Peter Dickinson's books—and my own Arthurian tales.

For all those who love Camelot, then, here is a book of ten fantastic stories and a song harkening back to the old days. Some of the stories are humorous, some glorious, some glamorous, some historical, and some quite tragic. Just as Arthurian stories *should* be: now and in the future.

Jane Yolen
Phoenix Farm

"I do beseech thee, Lord, that thou wilt permit Sir Ulfius and myself to presently convey the child away unto some place of safe refuge, where he may be hidden in secret until he groweth to manhood and is able to guard himself from such dangers as may threaten him."

Merlin at Arthur's birth
to King Uther Pendragon
from *The Story of King Arthur
and His Knights* by Howard Pyle

The Changing of the Shrew

Kathleen Kudlinski

"We will study planetary progression today, Arthur, because *that* is the lesson I have prepared." Merlin pushed a damp lock of gray hair off his forehead.

"But it's spring!" Arthur stood with his arms spread to catch the sunshine as it poured over the cold stone window sill. "Can't we just study spring, instead?"

The wizard looked over Arthur's shoulder at the first soft green on the far hillside pasture. "If you know the heavens well," he tried to tell the boy, "you'll know the seasons." Merlin wondered if the first fenny snakes were out basking in that warm sunshine. Curing a rash of winter fevers in the drafty castle had burned up nearly all of his snake tongues.

"Please, Merlin. For once can't we do something that isn't planned?"

"I suppose you'd rather play games," he said harshly. *But,*

Jove! it did sound good. This truly must be spring. "How about a race to the far hilltop?"

The boy's eyes reflected disbelief, then surprise, joy, then anger. "No fair. You'll fly!"

And that is what the wizard did. Spreading his arms wide, he placed the tips of his thumbs against the second joints of his third fingers. Humming a perfect A-flat, he stepped out through the window and drifted toward the kitchens below.

He flattered the cook into packing a hearty lunch for them, wheedled the dairy maid into giving up two crocks of buttermilk, and, floating on a lovely breeze up the hillside, charmed a dozen snakes into parting with their tongues. *A good morning's work,* he thought, shaking the cool spring air out from under his robes. But it had scarcely given him time to plan a lesson for a future king. *What to do with the boy?*

"Well, what shall we study?" Arthur panted as he finally crested the hill.

"Precisely." Merlin nodded sagely. "I thought we'd discuss it over lunch." He patted the cloth spread beside him, hoping the boy would sit quietly and let him think.

"Oh, Merlin. It's too early to eat. What can you show me about spring? Couldn't we do something magic?"

Why couldn't Arthur be in a growth spurt this spring, Merlin wondered, *instead of an intellectual stage?* He toyed with the idea of casting a growth spell, but decided against it. Cook hadn't packed enough food for that.

"Well?"

"All right, Arthur." Merlin was thinking on his feet, which was hard, for he was seated on the grass and quite

Humming a perfect A-flat, he stepped out through the window and drifted toward the kitchens below.

winded from his flight. *Spring fancies were for younger men,* he reminded himself. *Or should be.* "Perhaps I'll try something with you that I hadn't intended to do for several more years."

"I'm ready." Arthur plopped down beside the wizard.

"I'm not so sure you are. There may be some danger." As he heard his own words, Merlin could have kicked himself. A threat of danger never discouraged any ten-year-old.

Arthur jumped back to his feet, shouting "On with it, then!"

"Very well," Merlin said, though he knew that was not the case at all. "Listen closely for I shall not be with you after I cast the spell." Arthur quieted down as Merlin knew he would. He'd not used magic on the boy as yet, and it had frightened him. *As it should.*

"I am going to cast you into an animal's body. While you are there you must fend for yourself, for I cannot go with you."

Arthur clapped and shouted, "Oh, make me an eagle! Perhaps a lion? Or a stallion? . . ."

Merlin knew now he'd made an error. The boy was clearly too young, but it was too late to change courses. *What to do?*

"How about a griffon? Oh, could I be a dragon? Or maybe a . . ."

They both glanced down as a tiny animal scampered across the picnic cloth toward the cook's basket.

"A mouse!" Merlin roared, considerably relieved.

Arthur stopped in the middle of his heroic list. "You're going to make me into a mouse?"

"Yes. Do you have any questions?"

"Couldn't it be something more, well, grand?"

Merlin shook his head hoping the boy would decide to skip the whole lesson.

Arthur sat silently for a moment. "Will I be able to read the mouse's mind while I'm inside his body?"

"No. *His* mind will be in *your* body, beside me here on the picnic cloth." Merlin was beginning to regret the whole idea.

"So you get to talk to a giant mouse?" Arthur laughed aloud.

Merlin looked at the sky and began chanting.

As he finished the spell, Merlin watched the boy closely. Although Arthur looked the same to him, from his tangled brown hair to his worn leather boots, Merlin knew that a mouse's mind was taking over the strong young body. Soon the boy's muscles began to tremble. His eyes jerked wide open, and he jumped to his feet.

"Oh, my!" the mouse-in-Arthur whimpered as he tried to hide Arthur's body behind the lunch basket.

"Easy, easy," Merlin said gently. "I won't hurt you."

"But you are so big!" said the boy-shaped mouse, wringing his hands.

"Look at yourself, mouse. You, too, are big now." Moving slowly so he wouldn't frighten the timid animal, Merlin pointed toward Arthur's body. "I've played somewhat of a trick on you. You will be a boy for a few moments while I use your body for some magic."

The mouse-in-Arthur's eyes widened. When he opened his mouth, Merlin expected a yowl of terror. Instead, the giant mouse squeaked, and ran to hide behind a small tree.

"Really, now, old fellow," Merlin called to him. "There is nothing to worry about." The boy's shoulders stuck out on both sides of the sapling, but he did not move. "I'll protect you," Merlin promised.

Now Arthur's nose was visible on one side of the tree trunk. It was wiggling.

"I have some cheese in the basket," Merlin coaxed. "Come closer and I'll show you."

The mouse-in-a-boy hurried back, glancing over his shoulder as he came.

At the distant scream of a hawk, he grabbed the edge of the cloth and dove under it, upsetting the cheese, the sausage pasties, the wine, and the wizard.

Merlin sighed deeply and dusted off his robes. As he began picking up the scattered dinner, a whisper came through the cloth. "Do you have food?"

"Yes. Will you come out and share a bite?"

A moment passed and Merlin repeated his offer. "Did you hear me?" he asked the quivering cloth.

"Yes," the boy-shaped mouse whispered. "You mustn't speak so loudly. They'll find us."

"Who?" Merlin found himself whispering back.

"Don't jest about the Deaths," came the offended reply.

"Someone wants to kill you?" Merlin knew that Arthur's mind was somewhere near, planted in this mouse's tiny body. If that body died, so would Arthur. "Just how much danger is there for you?" he prodded.

The boy/mouse picked up the edge of the cloth and waved Merlin in. The old wizard looked around the field before he, too, climbed under the picnic cloth.

9

"The sky is full of danger," the mouse whispered in a sing-song voice. "Hawks and herons by day and owls by night. The grass crawls with danger: snakes and lizards and spiders." Merlin felt himself crouching further as he listened. "Danger pads on quiet paws: ferrets and weasels, badgers and foxes, cats and . . ." the mouse's whisper dropped to a hiss, " . . . shrews."

A cow mooed and the mouse-in-Arthur's-body stopped breathing.

"Are you all right?" Merlin whispered quickly.

The boy/mouse looked at him angrily and put his hand over Merlin's mouth.

When a few moments of silence had passed, the mouse continued, "The water swims with danger: bullfrogs and bass, turtles . . ."

"Don't mice think of anything besides being eaten?" Merlin wondered aloud.

"No," the mouse answered. "What else is there?"

"Enough!" Merlin shouted, throwing the cloth off their heads. He had to get the real Arthur back before he was eaten by one of these predators. As the mouse-in-Arthur's-body cowered in the grass at his feet, Merlin chanted the spell of undoing.

With the last words, the boy's body trembled. "Not now!" he whispered angrily. "I had almost reached the cheese in safety!"

Merlin looked at their picnic, once again spilled about on the grass.

"Oh, do get up," the wizard said. "We don't need to learn any more about mice."

"But I liked being small," Arthur answered. "I could hide anywhere."

"You kept yourself hidden?"

Arthur nodded emphatically. "It was so exciting to know there could be enemies everywhere. I still can feel that thrill."

Merlin wondered if he hadn't acted too quickly. Knowing how to hold a keen edge of caution could certainly help the future king in his court.

"Please make me a mouse again," Arthur begged. "I'll be perfectly safe." Merlin's eyebrows rose. "Well, I will be very careful. And I learned so much."

Merlin nodded, stroking his chin. They both had. "You want to be small again?"

Arthur nodded.

"But what shall you be? We must choose something safer than a mouse."

"Could I be a cat, Merlin? How about a falcon?"

"Hush, child, let me think." Which was the most dreaded animal on the mouse's list? Quiet and frightened, the mouse's voice came back to him: *"Badgers and foxes, cats and SHREWS."* That was it. "Would you like to learn about shrews?" he asked, though he already knew the answer.

"What a wonderful idea! They are bloody good fighters, Merlin. And they even have a poison bite. Can I start right off?"

Merlin again began the chant. Again there was no change to be seen in Arthur's body as the shrew's mind took over. As before, the eyes were the first clue that the change was complete. This time, they opened clear and alert. When they found Merlin, the shrew-in-Arthur's eyes narrowed.

"Oh, dear," muttered the wizard, backing off the cloth.

The boy-sized shrew sprang at him, caught his hand and sunk his teeth into Merlin's finger.

"Oh, do stop," Merlin cried. "This is all wrong." He tried to pull the boy's head away from his throbbing finger. The boy-sized shrew just ground his teeth in more deeply and watched Merlin's distress with obvious glee.

"Freeze!" Merlin shouted, and every living thing stopped. Bird song was stilled. The cows froze in place. Butterflies stopped flapping and fell to the soft grass. It was the only spell Merlin could think of on such short notice, and it hadn't quite solved the problem. He looked at the shrew-in-Arthur locked to his finger with astonishingly sharp teeth.

"Listen, shrew. You are, like it or not, a boy for a while. I am going to lift the spell and you will try to behave like a boy."

Merlin cast a release over the meadow. Bird and insect song filled the air. A rainbow's worth of butterflies flew up from the grasses. The cows again chewed their cud. And the shrew-in-Arthur gave one last crunch to the wizard's finger before he released his bite.

"Let's just sit here quietly, shrew, shall we? And wait for it all to be over." Merlin still didn't like the look in those wild eyes, but he was relieved to see the boy's body settling at the far corner of the picnic cloth.

"I am simply starving," said the shrew. "And you will provide my lunch."

"No, I think not," said Merlin. "Cook packed just enough for Arthur and me."

"You mistake me," said the shrew. "You've had your turn to hold me still. Now it is my turn." He pointed to Merlin's bloody finger. "My bite is poisonous. In moments you won't be able to move. It doesn't hurt to be eaten that way. At least none of my other victims have complained."

Merlin just smiled and waited.

The shrew-in-Arthur hummed tunelessly for a moment. "I am simply starving. Can you still move?" He looked hopefully at Merlin.

The magician raised his hand and waved at him.

"You know, if I don't eat every four hours, I shall die. I am quite truly starving. That is how we shrews are." He shrugged and looked hungrily at the cows grazing, then back at the wizard. "I say, aren't you feeling the least bit stiff yet?"

Merlin simply waved and grinned. "It is as I said. You are no more a shrew than I am. You are a boy."

The shrew-in-Arthur blinked once. "What do these boys eat?"

"For one thing, boys do not eat wizards." The idea left Merlin chuckling until he noticed the look on the shrew's face. He added firmly, "Never."

The wizard hoped this lesson was going more smoothly for his student. He had a sudden rush of affection for Arthur, a boy with such a quick, open mind and loving heart.

"Don't you ever think of anything besides eating?" he asked the shrew.

"No," the shrew answered. "What else is there?"

In the uneasy silence that followed, Merlin saw a tiny furry body in the grass beside the cloth. Before he could move he saw the shrew-in-Arthur grab the little animal and bite its head off.

Merlin yelped in surprise. Then he froze, staring at the small, headless body in horror. *What if the shrew-in-Arthur had just eaten Arthur-in-the-shrew? Was the real Arthur dead? What would become of Britain with this brutal creature as its king?*

"Mouse," the shrew-in-Arthur said, offering the limp, headless body to Merlin. "Care to try a bite?"

Merlin gagged and shook his head no. He watched, horrified, as the shrew-in-Arthur finished the morsel and picked his teeth. Finally he had to ask, "Are you sure that was a mouse?"

"Yes, quite. Meadow mouse, by the taste of it. Deer mice are sweeter. I'll catch that one over by the basket, if you'd like to try it."

"No!" cried Merlin. "Lessons are quite over for the morning." He raced through the spell of undoing.

At the last word, Arthur's glance darted quickly left, then right. "Where is that mouse!" he said. "I almost had him."

"Arthur," Merlin said gently. "We do not eat mice." He watched the boy's eyes cloud with confusion, then clear.

"I would actually have eaten a mouse?"

"Yes. Raw."

Arthur's face twisted and he swallowed hard. "I don't think I want to study any more today."

Merlin reached across the cloth and hugged the boy fiercely. Then they unpacked the cheeses, pasties, and buttermilk.

Arthur grabbed a morsel, crying, "I am simply starving!"

Merlin looked at him sharply. The boy grinned. "No, I guess I'm not *that* starving. But I'll never forget how real hunger feels." He appeared to be lost in thought. "Having a poison bite made everything different. It felt so powerful to know that if I could just make the first move, I would be in control of things. I wonder if that works with people, too?" His grin faded as he noticed the bloody tooth marks in Merlin's finger.

"The shrew, or rather, *I* did that to you?" he asked, in a tiny voice. And in a tinier voice, still, "I would actually have eaten you?"

"Yes. Raw." Merlin magicked away the wound and smiled kindly at the future king. "But you didn't."

Arthur was quiet a moment. "I guess that getting in the first move isn't a good idea until you're sure you're not hurting a friend."

Merlin nodded, then asked, "Would you mind if I don't plan this sort of lesson again for some time?"

"Fine." Arthur grinned at him. "Only Merlin, when we do study this way, shouldn't we hold the lessons *after* lunch?" Without waiting for an answer, he bit into the cheese.

He entered the wood and rejoiced to lie hidden under the ash trees; he marveled at the wild beasts feeding on the grass of the glades. . . . He lived on the roots of grasses and on the grass, on the fruit of the trees and on the mulberries of the thicket. . . . For a whole summer after this, hidden like a wild animal, he remained buried in the woods, found by no one and forgetful of himself and his kindred.

from *Vita Merlini* by
Geoffrey of Monmouth

Wild Man

Diana L. Paxson

"The wild men are coming! The wild men are coming!" a gaggle of children came shrieking past the booths where Queen Ganieda and her women were bargaining for glass beads. Lunet shifted the child in her arms and tried to see over his shoulder, but the Beltane drums were throbbing strongly up and down the dale, and the clearing below the dun was aswirl with folk come in for the festival.

Once, Lunet had loved the Festival of Beltane. She would chase as eagerly as those children after the wild men, or the Green Man, or the Horse. But that had been in the days before her father died in battle and her mother of sorrow, and she had been taken from their stronghold to live with strangers.

"Want to go!" cried the small boy she was trying to hold. "Cousin Lunet—want to *see*!"

"Wait, Morcant, we'll see them at the Maypole dancing, very soon . . ."

"Want to see them now!"

He drew breath with the little hiccup that always preceded his tantrums, his grubby fingers tangling her long brown hair, and Lunet jiggled him vigorously, flushing with embarrassment. It was bad enough that they had made her put on one of the queen's old gowns, which flapped upon her thin frame like the old clothes they hung on sticks to frighten the crows. If the child began to yell, everyone would stare at her.

"If you cause a fuss, your papa the king will be angry when he comes home from Luguvalium," she said desperately. "But your mama will give you sweets if you are a good boy!"

She looked up and met Queen Ganieda's sweet, weary smile, but it was old Elin who took the child from her arms, stopping the first yell with a firm hand. Morcant sputtered and his face reddened alarmingly.

"What is this, my small warrior?" the old woman said sternly. "Why, the wild men eat noisy little boys for their dinner!" She made a horrible gobbling sound deep in her throat and pretended to bite the boy's shoulder. His eyes rounded, and then he let out a little crow of laughter. "Come now, we will find a safe place and see!" Elin settled her charge upon her hip and turned to the queen.

"Let him look and then take him home," Ganieda said softly. "There is too much excitement for him here—" Her voice was controlled, as always, but in the queen's honey-brown eyes Lunet glimpsed tears.

For a moment she wondered why. Morcant's outburst was nothing unusual, and Elin would get him safely back to the dun.

"Let me go back with them," said Lunet as Elin started off, carrying the child whose care was the excuse they had used to get her down here and into these clothes.

"No—" said the queen. "Please, cousin, stay with me."

For a moment Lunet gazed wistfully at the stout earthen rampart on the hill above them and the top of the square Roman tower. There, she could get back into the boy's clothes she usually wore. The queen didn't care. It was the other women, clacking that she would never get a husband to help her rebuild her father's fortress if she did not look female, who had persuaded her into this gown. But she was afraid to go back to the place where her mother had died. And she certainly did not want a man.

The queen was still holding out her hand. Lunet moved to Ganieda's side, impatiently kicking the constraining skirts aside.

"Lady, these beads are lovely—" Bethoc exclaimed from the booth. "See how the red and yellow swirl through the glass."

"Roman work," said Julia Placidia, the one of Ganieda's ladies who clung most firmly to the old ways, though the Legions had departed from Britain fifty years before. "And old—see how the clasp is worn. The other pieces are the same. Where did this come from, old man?" She held up the necklace and the bright beads glittered in the sun.

"From the south, lady," came the reply in the accent of

Eburacum. "I had them honestly off a trader from Camulodo-
num, but I did not ask how he came by them."

"Has there been more fighting?" said Ganieda tremu-
lously. "Are the Saxons on the move again?"

"There's nought to fear, Lady," said the trader earnestly.
"It was not the Saxon wolves. They dare not raise their heads
since Verulamium!"

Lunet shivered, for the British had paid dearly for that
victory. Uther, the high king, had died and her own father
had died, and folk said that Queen Ganieda's brother Mirdyn
Ambrosius had been driven from his wits for misusing his
magic to help the British win.

"'Tis the Picts and the Scots that we should fear, and
praise heaven, they've been quiet this year," said Bethoc
quickly. One did not discuss that battle at Caer Gwenddolau,
but of course the trader could not know.

"Word is, these days they're fighting each other. Now it
is our own lords that make us afraid!" Julia Placidia answered her. "I have heard that the fighting in the south was
between two jumped-up British magnates who claim to be
kings." Julia sniffed. "It was not so in the days before the
legions left, or even when Vitalinus was acknowledged as
Vor-Tigern."

"A fine high king he was, who invited the Saxons in to
murder us all!" Bethoc replied.

"The Picts were at our gates, and he could not muster the
men to fight them. The Saxons would have served us faith-
fully if we had paid what we promised them," said Julia.
There was an uncomfortable silence.

"Well, what's past is done," said the trader briskly, "and these jewels will live anew with someone young and fair to wear them."

"I do not think so," said the queen, drawing the folds of her mantle over her coiled hair and turning away. "There is blood on them." Some of the women looked back at the glittering display with longing, but they followed her.

As they moved past the stands of the cloth sellers toward the meadow, the peals of raucous laughter and the shouting grew louder behind them.

"Are you well, lady?" asked Julia as the queen stumbled.

"Well enough to do my duty at this festival." Ganieda straightened, and Lunet took her arm, forgetting her own clumsiness. But as the queen's party moved on, the clamor behind them grew suddenly louder.

And then the wild men were upon them, brandishing blackthorn clubs or leafy wands and jumping with ear-splitting screeches into the air. Their limbs were covered by closefitting garments of rough cloth threaded thickly with yarn to give the appearance of fur—red, or yellow, or green, and they were crowned with leaves. Only their hands and feet and faces were bare. They were man-like in shape, but in those glaring eyes and flashing teeth Lunet recognized nothing of humanity.

One of them dropped suddenly in front of her, grimacing, and Lunet pushed him roughly away. Then a cry behind her brought her around. The queen had fallen. Julia was bending over her with the corner of her mantle clutched in her hand, fanning distractedly.

"Make a circle around her," cried Lunet. "Until they go away!"

It was no use trying to stir the wild men. They were a law unto themselves at the festivals, and the young men who were chosen for the role seemed to lose their human manners along with the tunics and braes they exchanged for their hairy coverings. But they rarely hurt people, unless someone tried to restrain them.

And indeed, in a few moments the whole wild troop went leaping away, swinging in a wide circle sunways around the meadow and leaving behind them shaken laughter and racing pulsebeats and the curious blend of fright and excitement that was their gift to the festival. She had forgotten how *alive* a visit from the wild men made everyone feel—

—Except for Queen Ganieda, who was weeping, and would neither explain nor be comforted.

"Do not think the wild men hurt me . . ." the queen said softly.

Now and then a whisper of music drifted up to the dun from the celebrations below, and the pulsebeat of drums still throbbed in the air. Lunet had volunteered to sit up with the queen when the other women went to bed. Ganieda's weakness worried her.

"The hurt that makes me weep is older."

"What do you mean?" Lunet poured mulled wine into the queen's cup of silver-bound polished horn. She was never clumsy when they were alone.

"My brother is a wild man . . . did not you know?"

The young men who were chosen for the role seemed to lose
their human manners . . .

Lunet paused with the earthenware wine jug poised in the air.

"Not like the lads who dress up and run about at fairs— a real one," said the queen.

"I heard that your brother was a sorcerer . . ." Lunet had discounted the wilder rumors as the sort of tale folk always told of those they served.

"My half-brother—" said the queen. "Ambros of Moridunon, whom they call Mirdyn, that my mother bore when she was still in the convent in Demetia. Some say a demon sired him, but the truth is stranger. My mother walked in the forest one day and lay down to sleep beneath an apple tree. She dreamed a wild man came and made love to her, and perhaps it was true, for she gave birth to a son ten moons later, and when he was born he was covered with hair. After that, of course, the holy women would have none of her. But my father was glad to get a daughter of the king of Demetia for his bride."

"But Mirdyn was no wild man when he served the high king!" Lunet exclaimed.

Ganieda laughed a little, the laughter of a small girl whose older brother has entertained her with miracles.

"Was he not? He was a master of earth-magic who spoke to the stones; who could sing the deer from the wood and the birds from the trees; a shape-changer and a weather-worker who drove the storms like unruly horses to do his will." On the hearth a log collapsed in a shower of sparks, and strange shadows chased each other across the white-washed wall.

"They say he played with powers unlawful for man to touch, at Verulamium . . ." Lunet said carefully. "And God made him mad."

"God? Perhaps," said the queen, "but when I remember what I have heard of that day—how he stood between the armies and saw the heavens riven and the warriors driven mad by the shapes he conjured until they slew themselves with their own swords—I think that his mind fled away from memory of what it is to be a man. Perhaps King Uther might have held him to humanity, but he was dead."

"Then why do you weep? It seems to me your Mirdyn must be happier without those memories!"

"You do not understand." Ganieda turned the cup between her slender fingers. "It is not my brother for whom I mourn, but for this land."

"Because of the fighting? But what could Mirdyn do to stop it? With no man left of the line of Maximus to rule them, the princes fight each other. Our people always do!"

"There is no man . . . but there is, if he still lives, a child." Ganieda gave a small, secret smile. "I have held him in my arms."

Lunet stared at her.

"Mirdyn brought King Uther to the Lady Igerna by magic before they were wed, and she bore him a son, but they feared for the child's safety, and so Mirdyn arranged for him to be fostered. I cared for the babe a few days before my brother took him to his new home, when I was no older than you."

"But where is he now?" Lunet exclaimed.

Ganieda shrugged, and laughed, and shrugged again. "Only my brother knows. . . ." She leaned back against the cushions, and the wine cup slipped from her hand.

Lunet frowned. The firelight was not kind, but she could no longer refuse to see how thin the queen had grown. Ganieda had never quite recovered from Morcant's birth—or had the trouble started earlier, after Verulamium?

She will die . . . the thought came as clearly as if someone had spoken. *If Mirdyn is not healed his sister will die, and this land will be destroyed as my home was destroyed when its defenders were gone!* But in that accounting, what weighed heaviest was that she would lose the only person who had cared about her since her parents died.

"Where is he?" Lunet said urgently. "Where is your brother now?"

"In the forests of the north. . . ." the queen murmured drowsily. "In Coed Caledon."

When Lunet was certain that Ganieda slept, she summoned the other women to put her to bed. But she sought her own bedplace only long enough to change into the boy's tunic that she wore when she roamed the fells, and to bind her blankets into a roll. In their place she left the gown that she had worn to the festival. Upon it she laid a spray of pine that someone had brought in with the Beltane greenery. Perhaps the queen would understand.

The great gate of Caer Gwenddolau was never opened until morning. But Lunet had not lived here for five years without learning where it was possible to climb from the top of a storage shed to the walkway, and where the smooth, sloping surface of the rampart had cracked enough for an active person to get down it and across the ditch to the gap in the secondary rampart beyond. King Rodarchus had been meaning to repair it, but there were always other tasks more needful, and so far the Picts had bypassed even so frayed a fortress in favor of easier prey.

When the sun rose she was trudging up Liddel Water, and by the time folk had recovered sufficiently from their Beltane revels to miss her, she was long gone. The bread and sausages that she had taken from the kitchens lasted her all the way up the dale, so there was no need to seek food at any steading where folk might remember a skinny lad with hacked-off brown hair. Two days' march brought her down from the fells into a land of thick forests, but the trees here were oak and ash. It was not the Forest of Caledon.

For the next two weeks Lunet pressed northward, pausing sometimes to use the skills she had learned from the herdboys and snare a woodcock or bring down a squirrel or a hare with her sling. Sometimes, too, she stopped at some isolated farmstead and worked long enough to earn the supplies to see her on her way. She avoided the duns, where someone might have wondered why a lad with the accent of the south was alone on the roads.

When she neared the great firth she turned westward, and north again where the Emperor Antoninus had tried once to make a wall to keep out the Painted People, and crossed into

Caledonia. She had cut herself a stout staff of rowanwood, good against evil, and got a leather scrip to carry her gear. The long miles up hill and down dale built muscle onto her thin frame, and the sun of early summer paled her hair as it was ripening the grain in the fields, and toasted her skin.

At the end of her third week of travel she came into a country of high hills cut by steepsided glens. Here were only single, palisaded farmsteads, and even they became less frequent as she went on. The oak forest was giving way to stands of pine, the outliers of the Great Caledonian Forest. From here to the shores that faced the furthermost isles the Forest ruled.

It was here that Lunet began to hear tales that set her ever more eagerly on her way. Of course there were wild men in the forest, said the folk who sheltered her. It was only in the south that they had become a legend. They walked like men but lived like beasts, and though they could be dangerous when frightened, they were not usually aggressive. But now there was one that could talk like a man. They called him Llalogan. He would appear, laughing madly, at dun or farmstead, his bodyfur matted and his long hair and beard all stuck with twigs like the nest of a bird. Sometimes he sang, or muttered riddles that none could understand.

Llalogan came once to Dun Durn, they said, when their chieftan Meldred was there. The warriors made sport of him, and the women laughed and threw him food, until someone realized that the wild man's nonsense had just revealed the queen's adultery.

Lunet heard that story as she sat by a cowherd's fire all through one long northern twilight, eating hard bread and cheese.

"But Grisandole is the queen, see you," said the old man, "and though Meldred might like to follow southern ways, he only rules because of her. He dares not divorce her, so for revenge he hunts the wild man. But though the king has sent men to beat the Forest, they have found only the voiceless wild men there. Llalogan still turns up sometimes, laughing, with a little pig running by his side. He has riddled that he can be caught only by one who is neither kin nor stranger, neither man nor woman, neither young nor old." The man cackled with laughter, and took another drink of heather-beer.

"Where did they see him last, then?" Lunet asked softly.

"Now don't ye be getting curious!" The old man wagged his finger in Lunet's face and she flinched from his sour breath. "I know lads, I do. Tear ye limb from limb soon as look at ye, he would. You stay away from Lake Earn!"

The herdsman settled back, mumbling, and soon he was snoring. But Lunet stayed long awake. If this wild man was not Mirdyn, where could she go? Could she, who was a riddle to herself sometimes, solve the riddle of Llalogan?

The whisper of wind in the pines was incessant, as if the trees themselves were mocking her. Lunet looked over her shoulder and in the next moment stubbed her toe on a rock and stopped, swearing. There was nothing behind her—not this time, not any of the times she had been certain she was being watched before. Perhaps the pines really were passing the word of her coming from tree to tree as she stumbled on.

She had come fully into the domain of the Forest. Where young trees were still striving to establish themselves, the ground was dark even at noonday. But where mature pines grew more sparsely the earth might be covered by a brilliant green carpet of moss, or on the higher slopes, with heather and bilberries. Sometimes the pines shared the ground with silver birch or shapely rowan, and where the bald crowns of the hills broke through the trees, sturdy junipers clung to the scree.

She had almost lost hope of finding the wild man, or even Lake Earn. After two days of wandering, she would have been happy to find *anything,* even a herder's hut, in this wilderness.

She leaned on her staff, wiggling her toe. Somewhere below she could hear the musical rush of water over stone. Her stomach growled hopefully and she suppressed awareness of hunger. At least she could drink, and perhaps there would be tender fern shoots or sweet herbs near the stream. Her toe had almost stopped hurting. Cautiously, she started down the hill.

The ground was criss-crossed with tracks where the sandy soil had been kept moist by the spray. Lunet scanned the slope, seeking the print of the wolf she had heard howling the night before, and found the round padmark of a wildcat, the paired wedge-shaped imprints of red deer, and crossing them, a mark that was similar, but broader. Her pulse began to race as she realized that she was looking at a pig's track stamped into the soft ground.

Even a sorcerer could not keep a pig from leaving prints, or forever hide his own. Where fallen needles had made a rich mulch she found a single impression of a man's foot with long, splayed toes. At the edge of a thickly-wooded corrie she found another, and then more of them. But the new prints were larger, set too far apart for any human stride. Lunet stopped, staring. It was then that she began to be afraid.

But she would rather face the wild men than Ganieda's despair.

Trembling, she followed what had become a well-defined trail along the stream. Through the trees she glimpsed the sheen of water like a polished sword. It took her a moment to realize that the lake was visible because this had once been a clearing, though young trees were already sprouting in the yard, and of the house only a circle of rotting timbers remained.

The pig was rooting industriously at the foot of the other thing that men had left here—a gnarled apple tree.

Lunet moved slowly forward. Something rustled among the leaves and her breath caught. She looked upward, and glimpsed a pair of honey-brown, human eyes.

"Ambros—Llalogan—" her voice squeaked. "I've come from your sister. It's time to come home."

A peal of wild laughter shook the air and the branches shivered violently, but the eyes did not reappear. Abruptly Lunet's strength left her, and she slid to the ground at the foot of the apple tree.

She had done it, she had found him! And he was mad. *Never mind.* Lunet thought dismally, too exhausted to move. *As soon as I starve you can come down!* She closed her eyes.

She must have slept then, for when she was aware once more, sunset was flaming behind the trees. A rustle from above told her that her captive was still there, but they were not alone. Hunkered down in a circle, watching her, were the wild men. At her movement they flickered back among the trees. But they did not go far. Moving shadows among the tree-trunks kept her tense until she realized that they too were afraid.

If she left the tree, her captive would disappear. She called to him again, but there was no response, and presently, she slept once more. In her dreams, it seemed to her that the trees were talking.

"Drop your branches on her head; smother her with leaves! She comes to steal the Guardian!" hissed the pine trees, and the birches echoed, "Sweep her away . . ."

But the apple tree answered them, "She has sought my protection, and so has he. Those who eat my fruit shall live. . . ."

In the morning, she saw a pile of early bilberries placed just out of reach. Were they meant for Mirdyn? Lunet divided them into two piles. She tossed a spray up into the leaves and it fell back to the ground, but the second disappeared.

After a time the wild men began to venture out from among the trees. She counted two females, one of them with a cub, a half-grown male and another in his prime. They seemed to live on roots and leaves and berries, on grubs and insects they found in the bark of trees. Lunet and her captive lived on them too. She found that a quick dash to the steam would fill her cup before Mirdyn could get out of the tree. After that, she filled her waterskin and hung it on one of the lower branches and she saw a brown, hair-covered hand reach down for it.

On the first day, she heard a strange, wordless singing from the top of the tree. On the second day, there were words in it, though in no language that she knew. On the third day she was awakened by a lullabye she had heard Ganieda sing to her child. At her movement, the voice faltered, and Lunet finished the verse.

The honey-bee shall give thee gold,
The lamb's white fleece keep thee from cold,
The arms of the mother the child safe hold!

There was a silence.

"Listen, wild man," she said finally. "I am a niece of Ganieda's father, and so I'm kin but not blood-kin to you; and I am a girl, though I wear boy's clothes; no child, but not likely to be a wife, for who would have me? So I've caught you."

"I am a man without memory. I am a beast without innocence. I am the cursed one. Let me alone!"

Lunet shivered. His voice was deep, as if the earth had spoken, but it rang like a cracked bell.

"Does that matter?" she said. "You are needed in the world of men."

32

There was silence above her, and she settled herself to wait once more. That night she dreamed that the beasts of the wood came out from among the trees; the red stag and the grey hare, wolf and wildcat and bear. They sat debating like a king's counselors in a circle around the apple tree.

"Seize the maiden in your strong jaws! Drag her into the Forest, tear her to shreds. She comes to take the Lord of Beasts away!"

"She is my daughter, as he is my son—" said the piglet, but now it was a black sow, huge and terrible. "When they know that, they will be free."

All through the next day, and during the days that followed, Lunet talked. She talked about the people and the places she had seen during her journey. She talked about what would happen to Britain if no one brought peace to the land. She talked about old Elin, and little Morcant, and Caer Gwenddolau.

On the sixth night she dreamed that the wild folk came into the clearing, and they were weeping as the women weep when the warriors march away.

"Do not leave us, brother! Who will lead us if you are gone? Let us take her out of the forest. Do not let her lure you away!"

The answer this time seemed to come from above her.

"You cannot touch her. Her power is that of the pure in spirit. Why will she not set me free?"

Lunet woke, wondering. The wild men were sitting as she had dreamed them, grooming each other or hunting bugs beneath the leaves, and watching her sadly. Had she dreamed true, or was it her weakness that read meaning into those dark eyes? When she went to the stream for water her head spun dizzily.

No wonder the saints who fast in the wilderness have visions, she thought as she sat down again. *I'm no longer sure myself what is real!*

"Everyone knows that if the princes cannot stop fighting each other, the Saxons will eat us all," she spoke to the tree. "Ganieda says that King Uther had a son, and you hid him away. If he could be found, they would obey him, and give us peace again."

"He is safe where he is . . ." came the harsh answer from above her. "If he is made king, there will be more battles! More . . . bloody . . . war!"

For three days, they argued about it.

"People can face danger if there is a reason for it," Lunet said at last. "I made it here! But the suffering has to mean something, and not knowing who you are can be the worst of all. That boy is the son of Uther Pendragon! He must feel like an eaglet in a nest of daws! But unless you find him, he will never know why! I don't fit in anywhere either, not since my parents died. But at least I know who they were!"

There was a subtle change in the quality of the silence. Somehow it had gotten dark, and when Mirdyn replied it was as if the night itself was saying the words.

"There was once a boy who was born different. The other children threw stones at him and called him beast. And then

34

one day he summoned a wolf out of the forest, and it killed three of them before they ran away . . . .

"Once there was a youth who had no father." Now the voice was stronger. "The people of his village sold him to the high king's magicians to be sacrificed, but he saw the dragon-powers moving through the earth beneath the king's tower, and when they dug down they found a pool, and the power flowed outward into the land." The words beat at her awareness.

"Once there was a man whose lord was slain. And he used his powers to rip asunder the veils between the worlds, and those who saw it went mad and died. . . ." The words disintegrated into anguished laughter.

"Who is that boy, that youth, that man?" the wild man cried. "Where does he belong? In the Forest, the beasts do not reproach him, and he saves more than he slays."

"If you return, you will save men," said Lunet. "Bring Uther's son to his father's high seat and no one will question your wisdom!"

"Will they not?" More laughter scored the soft air. "I see all futures from this apple tree. If that child becomes high king, his fame will never die. But that will not preserve him from sorrow, for in the end those he loves best will betray him. What thanks will he give me then?"

"All men have sorrow!" Lunet beat the ground in frustration. "Do you think you are the only one who ever suffered, Mirdyn? All you say may be true. I know only that if you don't go home, Ambros Mirdyn, your sister is going to die. And I love her, I need her. . . ." Something that had been tight-braced to endurance inside her snapped then, and suddenly Lunet was weeping wildly, her head upon her knees.

The branches above her thrashed violently, and there was a soft thunder of falling objects that battered her head and shoulders and bounced away. Blinking through her tears, Lunet realized that she could see them. Around her, the world was slowly taking form from the mists of dawn. The things that had hit her were apples. They were still hard and small, but on some of the shiny green skins the first blush of ripeness showed.

She picked up one of them, staring at it as if she had never seen one before. Wondering, she bit into it, just where the red side met the green, and gasped as a wave of tart sweetness turned all her perceptions upside down. For a moment she was part of the soil, and the sky, the life of the tree and that of the man it bore.

"Mirdyn, I do not care what you are!" she cried. "Come to me!"

The tree groaned as the lower branches took his weight, and more leaves showered to the ground. And then he was falling earthward like some last unseasonable fruit. She tried to steady him, but when he came to rest his limbs were strengthless as a new lamb's. She pulled his head into her lap and looked down at him.

He was bigger than she had expected, scratched and scarred, the shape of his bones showing through the wiry brown hair that grew so thickly on his hide. Hair and beard were brown also, sun-streaked and matted into long cords like felted wool. But they were not the thick, glossy pelt of the wild folk, and when he finally opened them, the wild amber eyes were those of a man.

From among the trees, the wild folk watched them. Lunet recognized the mute reproach in their eyes, and turned her gaze quickly back to her strange captive.

"Will you come with me?" She stroked the weather-browned skin of his brow. Mirdyn sighed.

"If I return to the world I will do good and evil, and in the end they will kill me. They will beat me with staves and pierce me with a spear. In the end I will be drowned."

Lunet bit her lip, sensing the weight of the burden that he was taking up once more. Unbelievably, she had won her battle, and suddenly she began to understand the terrible responsibilities of victory. A little desperately, she picked up one of the apples and put it into his hand. He looked at it as she had, and then he bit into the side that was ripening.

"It does not matter," he whispered presently. "I will have peace then, and the land will take me back again . . ."

"You will go to seek Uther's son?"

"I will go . . . sister . . . and you?"

The knowledge of what she must do came to her suddenly. There were people there, at her old home, who depended on her family for their safety as surely as Britain depended on the line of the kings.

"I will ask Ganieda for men and supplies, and rebuild my father's dun . . ."

He sat up, as if the apple had been some magic to give him his strength again. Painfully, Lunet got to her feet beside him. The pig was already trotting up the path beside the stream.

Slowly, Lunet and Mirdyn Ambrosius followed. Behind them, the wild folk faded into the mists of morning and disappeared.

. . . when matins were done the congregation filed out to the yard. They were confronted by a marble block into which had been thrust a beautiful sword. The block was four feet square, and the sword passed through a steel anvil which had been struck in the stone, and which projected a foot from it. The anvil had been inscribed with letters of gold:

WHOSO PULLETH OUTE THIS SWERD
OF THIS STONE AND ANVYLD
IS RIGHTWYS KYNGE
BORNE OF ALL BRYTAYGNE.

from *Le Morte d' Arthur* by
Sir Thomas Malory

Once and Future

Terry Pratchett

The copper wire. It was the copper wire that gave me the trouble.

It's all down to copper wire. The old alchemists used to search for gold. If only they'd known what a man and a girl can do with copper wire . . .

And a tide mill. And a couple of hefty bars of soft iron.

And here I am now, with this ridiculous staff in one hand and the switch under my foot, waiting.

I wish they wouldn't call me Merlin. It's Mervin. There *was* a Merlin, I've found out. A mad old guy who lived in Wales and died years ago. But there were legends about him, and they're being welded onto me now. I reckon that happens all the time. Half the famous heroes of history are really lots of local guys all rolled into one by the ballad singers. Remember Robin Hood? Technically I suppose I can't, because none of the rascals who went under that name will be born for several centuries yet, if he even is due to exist in this universe, so using the word *remember* is probably the wrong, you know, grammar. Can you remember something that hasn't happened yet? I can. Nearly everything I can remember hasn't happened yet, but that's how it goes in the time travel business. Gone today and here tomorrow . . .

Oh. Here comes another one of them. A strapping lad. Legs like four beer kegs stacked in pairs, shoulders like an ox. Brain like an ox too, I shouldn't wonder. Hand like a bunch of bananas, gripping the sword. . . .

Oh, no, my lad. You're not the one. Grit your teeth all you like. You're not the one.

There he goes. His arm'll be aching for days.

You know, I suppose I'd better tell you about this place. About this *time*.

Whenever it is . . .

I had special training for time travelling. The big problem, the *big* problem, is finding out *when* you are. Basically, when you step out of a time machine you can't rely on seeing a little sign that says "Welcome to 500 AD, Gateway to the Dark Ages, pop. 10 million and falling." Sometimes you can't even rely on finding anyone in a day's march who *does* know what year it is, or what king is on the throne, or what a king *is*. So you learn to look at things like church architecture, the way the fields are farmed, the shape of the ploughshares, that sort of thing.

Yeah, I know, you've seen films where there's this dinky little alpha-numeric display that tells you exactly where you are . . .

Forget it. It's all dead reckoning in this game. Real primitive stuff. You start out by checking the constellations with a little gadget, because they tell me all the stars are moving around all the time and you can get a very rough idea of when you are just by looking through the thing and reading off along the calibrations. If you can't even *recognize* the constellations, the best thing to do is run and hide, because something forty feet tall and covered with scales is probably hunting you already.

Plus they give you a guide to various burned-out supernovas and Stofler's Craters of the Moon by Estimated Creation Date. With any luck you can pinpoint yourself fifty years either way. Then it's just a matter of checking planetary positions for the fine tuning. Try to imagine sea navigation around the time of, oh, Columbus. A bit hit-or-miss, yeah? Well, time navigation is just about at the same level.

Everyone said I must be one great wizard to spend so much time studying the sky.

That's because I was trying to find out where I *was*.

Because the sky tells me I'm around 500 AD. So why is the architecture Norman and the armour fifteenth century?

Hold on . . . here comes another one . . .

Well, not your actual Einstein, but it could be . . . oh, no, look at that grip, look at that *rage* . . . no. He's not the one. Not him.

Sorry about that.

So . . . right . . . where was I? Memory like a sieve these days.

Yeah, the architecture. And everyone speaking a sort of Middle English, which was okay as it turned out because I can get by in that, having accidentally grounded in 1479 once. That was where I met John Gutenberg, father of modern printing. Tall man, bushy whiskers. Still owes me tuppence.

Anyway. Back to *this* trip. It was obvious from the start that things weren't quite right. This time they were supposed to be sending me to observe the crowning of Charlemagne in 800 AD, and here I was in the wrong country and, according to the sky, about three centuries too soon. That's the kind of thing that happens, like I said; it's going to be at least fifty years before we get it right. Fifty-three years, actually, because I met this man in a bar in 1875 who's from a hundred years in our future, and he told me. I told them at Base we might as well save a lot of effort by just, you know, bribing one of the future guys for the plans of the next model. They said if we violated the laws of Cause-and-Effect like that there's a good chance the whole universe would suddenly catastrophically collapse into this tiny bubble .005 Ångstroms across, but I say it's got to be worth a try.

Anyway, the copper wire gave me a load of trouble.

That's not to say I'm an incompetent. I'm just an average guy in every respect except that I'm the one in ten thousand who can time travel and still end up with all his marbles. It just gives me a slight headache. And I'm good at languages and I'm a very good observer, and you'd better believe I've observed some strange things. The Charlemange coronation was going to be a vacation. It was my second visit, paid for by a bunch of historians in some university somewhere. I was going to check a few things that the guys who commissioned

the first trip had raised after reading my report. I had it all
worked out where I was going to stand so I wouldn't see
myself. I could probably have talked my way out of it even
if I *had* met myself, at that. One thing you learn in this
trade is the gift of the gab.

And then a diode blew or a one turned out to be a zero
and here I am, whenever this is.

And I can't get back.

Anyway . . . what was I saying . . .

Incidentally, the other problem with the copper wire is
getting the insulation. In the end I wrapped it up in fine
cloth and we painted every layer with some sort of varnish
they use on their shields, which seems to have done the trick.

And . . . hmm . . . you know, I think time travelling
affects the memory. Like, your memory subconsciously knows
the things you're remembering haven't happened yet, and
this upsets it in some way. There's whole bits of history I
can't remember. Wish I knew what they were.

Excuse me a moment. Here's another one. An oldish guy.
Quite bright, by the look of him. Why, I bet he can probably write his own name. But, oh, I don't know, he hasn't
got the . . .

Hasn't got the . . .

Wish I knew what it was he hasn't got . . .

. . . *charisma*. Knew it was there somewhere.

So. Anyway. Yeah. So there I was, three centuries adrift,
and nothing working. Ever seen a time machine? Probably
not. The bit you move around is very, very hard to see, unless the light catches it just right. The actual works are back

45

at Base and *at the same time* in the machine, so you travel in something like a mechanical ghost, something like what's left of a machine when you take all the parts away. An *idea* of a machine.

Think of it as a big crystal. That's what it'd look like to you if, as I said, the light was right.

Woke up in what I suppose I've got to call a bed. Just straw and heather with a blanket made of itches woven together. And there was this girl trying to feed me soup. Don't even try to imagine medieval soup. It's made of all the stuff they wouldn't eat if it was on a plate and believe me, they'd eat stuff you'd hate to put in a hamburger.

I'd been there, I found out later, for three days. I didn't even *know* I'd arrived. I'd been wandering around in the woods, half-conscious and dribbling. A side-effect of the travelling. Like I said, normally I just get a migraine, but from what I can remember of *that* it was jet-lag times one million. If it had been winter I'd have been dead. If there'd been cliffs I would have thrown myself over one. As it was, I'd just walked into a few trees, and that was by accident. At least I'd avoided the wolves and bears. Or maybe they'd avoided me, maybe they think you die if you eat a crazy person.

Her father was a woodcutter, or a charcoal burner, or one of those things. Never did find out, or perhaps I did and I've forgotten. He used to go out every day with an axe, I remember that. He'd found me and brought me home. I learned afterward he thought I was a nobleman, because of my fine clothes. I was wearing Levi's, that should give you some idea. He had two sons, and they went out every day with axes, too. Never really managed to strike up a conversation with

46

either of them until after the father's accident. Didn't know enough about axes, I suppose.

But Nimue . . . What a girl. She was only . . . er . . .

"How old were you, when we met?"

She wipes her hands on a bit of rag. We'd had to grease the bearings with pig fat.

"Fifteen," she says. "I think. Listen, there's another hour of water above the mill, but I don't think the gennyrator will last that long. It's shaking right merrily."

She looks speculatively at the nobles.

"What a bunch of by-our-Lady jacks," she says.

"Jocks."

"Yes. Jocks."

I shrug. "One of them will be your king," I tell her.

"Not *my* king, Mervin. I will never have a king," she says, and grins.

By which you can tell she's learned a lot in twelve months. Yes, I broke the rules and told her the truth. And why not? I've broken all the rules to save this damn country, and it doesn't look like the universe is turning into this tiny ball .005 Ångstroms across. First, I don't think this is *our* time line. It's all wrong, like I said. I think I was knocked sideways, into some sort of other history. Maybe a history that'll never really exist except in people's heads, because time travel is a fantasy anyway. You hear mathematicians talk about imaginary numbers which are real, so I reckon this is an imaginary place made up of real things. Or something. How should I know? Perhaps enough people believing something makes it real.

I'd ended up in Albion, although I didn't find out until

47

later. Not Britain, not England. A place very much like them, a place that shares a lot of things with them, a place so close to them that maybe ideas and stories leak across— but a place that is its own place.

Only something went wrong somewhere. There was some-one missing. There should have been a great king. You can fill in his name. He's out there somewhere, in the crowd. It's lucky for him I turned up.

You want me to describe this world. You want to hear about the jousts, the pennants, the castles. Right. It's got all of that. But everything else has this, like, thin film of mud over it. The difference between the average peasant's hut and a pigsty is that a good farmer will sometimes change the straw in a pigsty. Now, get me right—no one's doing any repressing, as far as I can see. There's no slavery as such, except to tradition, but tradition wields a heavy lash. I mean, maybe democracy isn't perfect, but at least we don't let our-selves be outvoted by the dead.

And since there's no strong man in charge there's a little would-be king in every valley, and he spends most of his time fighting other would-be kings, so the whole country is in a state of half-hearted war. And everyone goes through life proudly doing things clumsily just because their forefathers did them that way, and no one really enjoys anything, and good fields are filling with weeds . . .

I told Nimue I came from another country, which was true enough.

I talked to her a lot because she was the only one with any sense around the place. She was small, and skinny, and

48

alert in the same way that a bird is alert. I said I broke the rules to save this country but if I'm honest, I'll have to say I did it all for her. She was the one bright thing in a world of mud, she's nice to have around, she learns quickly, and— well, I've seen what the women here look like by the time they're thirty. That shouldn't happen to anyone.

She talked and she listened to me while she did the housework, if that's what you can call moving the dirt around until it got lost.

I told her about the future. Why not? What harm could it do? But she wasn't very impressed. I guess she didn't know enough to *be* impressed. Men on the moon were all one with the fairies and the saints. But piped water caught her interest, because every day she had to go to a spring with a couple of wooden buckets on a yoke thing round her neck.

"Every cottage has this?" she said, eyeing me carefully over the top of the broom.

"Sure."

"Not just the rich?"

"The rich have more bathrooms," I said. Then I had to explain about bathrooms.

"You people could do it," I told her. "You just need to dam a spring up in the hills, and find a—a blacksmith or someone to make some copper pipes. Or lead or iron, at a pinch."

She looked wistful.

"My father wouldn't allow it," she said.

"Surely he'd see the benefits of having water laid on?" I suggested.

She shrugged. "Why should he? He doesn't carry it from the spring."

"Oh."

But she took to following me around, in what time there was between chores. It's just as I've always said—women have always had a greater stake in technology than have men. We'd still be living in trees, otherwise. Piped water, electric lighting, stoves that you don't need to shove wood into—I reckon that behind half the great inventors of history were their wives, nagging them into finding a cleaner way of doing the chores.

Nimue trailed me like a spaniel as I tottered around their village, if you could use the term for a collection of huts that looked like something deposited in the last Ice Age, or possibly by a dinosaur with a really serious bowel problem. She even let me into the forest, where I finally found the machine in a thorn thicket. Totally unrepairable. The only hope was that someone might fetch me, if they ever worked out where I was. And I knew they never would, because if they *ever* did, they'd have been there *already*. Even if it took them ten years to work it out, they could still come back to the Here and Now. That's the thing about time travel; you've got all the time in the world.

I was marooned.

However, we experienced travellers always carry a little something to tide us over the bad times. I'd got a whole box of stuff under the seat. A few small gold ingots (acceptable everywhere, like the very best credit cards). Pepper (worth more than gold for hundreds of years). Aluminum (a rare and precious metal in the days before cheap and plentiful electricity). And seeds. And pencils. Enough drugs to start a store. Don't tell me about herbal remedies—people screamed down the centuries, trying to stop things like dental abscesses with any green junk that happened to be growing in the mud.

She watched me owlishly while I sorted through the stuff and told her what it all did.

And the next day her father cut his leg open with his axe. The brothers carried him home. I stitched him up and, with her eyes on me, treated the wound. A week later he was walking around again, instead of being a cripple at best or most likely a gangrenous corpse, and I was a hero. Or, rather, since I didn't have the muscles for a hero, obviously a wizard.

I was mad to act like that. You're not supposed to meddle. But what the hell. I was *marooned*. I was never going *home*. I didn't *care*. And I could cure, which is almost as powerful as being able to kill. I taught hygiene. I taught them about turnips, and running water, and basic medicine.

The boss of the valley was a decent enough old knight called Sir Ector. Nimue knew him, which surprised me, but shouldn't have. The old boy was only one step up from his peasants, and seemed to know them all, and wasn't much richer than they were except that history had left him with a crumbling castle and a suit of rusty armour. Nimue went up to the castle one day a week to be a kind of lady's maid for his daughter.

After I pulled the bad teeth that had been making his life agony, old Ector swore eternal friendship and gave me the run of the place. I met his son Kay, a big hearty lad with the muscles of an ox and possibly the brains of one, and there was this daughter to whom no one seemed to want to introduce me properly, perhaps because she was very attractive in a quiet kind of way. She had one of those stares that seems to be reading the inside of your skull. She and Nimue got along like sisters. Like sisters that get along well, I mean.

I became a big man in the neighborhood. It's amazing the impression you can make with a handful of medicines, some basic science, and a good line in bull.

Poor old Merlin had left a hole which I filled like water in a cup. There wasn't a man in the country who wouldn't listen to me.

And whenever she had a spare moment Nimue followed me, watching like an owl.

I suppose at the time I had some dream, like the Connecticut Yankee, of single-handedly driving the society into the twentieth century.

You might as well try pushing the sea with a broom.

"But they do what you tell them," Nimue said. She was helping me in the lab at the time, I think. I call it the lab, it was just a room in the castle. I was trying to make penicillin.

"That's exactly it," I told her. "And what good is that? The moment I turn my back, they go back to the same old ways."

"I thought you told me a dimocracy was where people did what they wanted to do," she said.

"It's a democracy," I said. "And it's fine for people to do what they want to do, provided they do what's right."

She bit her lip thoughtfully. "That does not sound sensible."

"That's how it works."

"And when we have a, a democracy, every man says who shall be king?"

"Something like that, yes."

"And what do the women do?"

I had to think about that. "Oh, they should have the vote, too," I said. "Eventually. It'll take some time. I don't think Albion is ready for female suffrage."

"It has female sufferage already," she said, with unusual bitterness.

"*Suffrage.* It means the right to vote."

I patted her hand.

"Anyway," I told her, "you can't start with a democracy. You have to work up through stuff like tyranny and monarchy first. That way people are so relieved when they get to democracy that they hang onto it."

"People used to do what the king told them," she said, carefully measuring bread and milk into the shallow bowls. "The high king, I mean. Everyone did what the high king said. Even the lesser kings."

I'd heard about this high king. In his time, apparently, the land had flowed with so much milk and honey people must have needed waders to get around. I don't go for that kind of thing. I'm a practical man. When people talk about their great past they're usually trying to excuse the mediocre present.

"Such a person might get things done," I said. "But then they die, and history shows"—or *will* show, but I couldn't exactly put it like that to her—"that things go back to being even worse when they die. Take it from me."

"Is that one of those things you call a figure of speech, Mervin?"

"Sure."

"There was a child, they say. Hidden somewhere by the king until it was old enough to protect itself."

"From wicked uncles and so on?"

"I do not know about uncles. I heard men say that many kings hated the power of Uther Pendragon." She stacked the dishes on the windowsill. I really hadn't got much idea about penicillin, you understand. I was just letting stuff go mouldy, and hoping.

"Why are you looking at me like that?" she said.

"Uther Pendragon? From Cornwall?"

"You knew him?"

"I—er—I—yes. Heard of him. He had a castle called Tintagel. He was the father of—"

She was staring at me.

I tried again. "He was a king here?"

"Yes!"

I didn't know what to say to her. I wandered over to the window and looked out. There was nothing much out there but forest. Not clear forest, like you'd find Tolkien's elves in, but deep, damp forest, all mosses and punk-wood. It was creeping back. Too many little wars, too many people dying, not enough people to plough the fields. And out there, somewhere, was the true king. Waiting for his chance, waiting for—

Me?

I was trying to make penicillin.

The king. Not any old king. The *king.* Arthur. Artos the Bear. Once and Future. Round Table. Age of Chivalry. He never existed.

Except here. Maybe.

Maybe *here,* in a world you get to in a broken time machine, a world that's not exactly history and not exactly memory and not exactly story . . .

And I was the only one who knew how the legend went. Me. Mervin.

With his leadership and my, er, experience . . . what a team . . .

I looked at her face. Clear as a pond now, but a little worried. She was thinking that old Mervin was going to be ill again.

I remember I drummed my fingers on the cold windowsill. No central heating in the castle. Winter was coming. It was going to be a bad one, in this ruined country.

Then I said, "Ooooooh."

She looked startled.

"Just practicing," I said, and tried again. "Oooo*ooooo*oooh, hear me, hear me." Not bad, not bad. "Hear me, o ye men of Albion, hear me. It is I, Mervin, that's with a V, who speaks to you. Let the message go out that a Sign has been sent to end the wars and choose the rightwise King of Albion . . . *Oooooooooo*h-er."

She was near to panic by this time. A couple of servants were peering around the door. I sent them away.

"How was it?" I said. "Impressive, eh? Could probably work, yeah?"

"What is the Sign?" she whispered.

55

"Traditionally, a sword in a stone," I said. "Which only the rightful heir can pull out."

"But how can that *be?*"

"I'm not sure. I'll have to think of a way."

That was months ago.

The obvious way was some sort of bolt mechanism or something . . .

No, of course I didn't think there was a mystic king out there. I kept telling myself that. But there was a good chance that there was a lad who maybe looked good on a horse and was bright enough to take advice from any wizardly types who happened to be around. Like I said, I'm a practical man.

Anyway . . . what was I saying? Oh, yes. All the mechanical ways of doing it I had to rule out. That left electricity. Strange thing is, it's a lot easier to make a crude electrical generator than a crude steam engine. The only really critical things are the bearings.

And the copper wire.

It was Nimue who eventually sorted that one out.

"I've seen ladies wearing fine jewelry with gold and silver wires in it," she said. "The men who made them must know how to do it with copper."

And of course she was right. I just wasn't thinking straight. They just pulled thin strips of metal through tough steel plates with little holes in them, gradually bullying it into smaller and smaller thickness. I went to London and found a couple who could do it, and then I got a blacksmith to make up some more drawplates because I didn't want wire in jewelry quantities but in industrial amounts. I'd already

56

got quite a reputation then, and no one asked me what I needed it for. I could have said, "Well, half will be for the generator, and the rest will be for the electromagnets in the stone," and what would they have known? I had another smith make me up the soft iron cores and the bearings, and Nimue and I spent hours winding the wire and shellacking every layer.

The motive power was the easy part. The country was thick with mills. I chose a tide mill, because it's dependable and this one was on an impressive stretch of coast. I know the legend said it was done in London or Winchester or some place, but I had to go where the power was and, anyway, it looked good, there on the shore with the surf pounding on the rocks and everything.

The stone was the easy bit. There's been a crude concrete technology ever since the Romans. Though I say it myself, I made quite a nice-looking stone around the electromagnets. We got it finished days before the day I'd set for the big contest. We'd put up a big canvas shield around it, although I don't think any of the locals would have come near it for a fortune.

Nimue operated the switch while I slid the sword in and out.

"That means you're king," she said, grinning.

"Not me. I haven't got what it takes to rule."

"Why? What does it take?"

"We'll know when we see it. We're looking for a boy with the air of authority. The kind of lad a war-weary people will follow."

"And you're sure you'll find him?"

57

"If I don't, the universe isn't being run properly."

She's got this funny way of grinning. Not exactly mock-ing, but it's always made me feel uneasy.

"And he'll listen to you?"

"He'd better. I'm the wizard round here. There's not a man in the country I can't out-think, my girl."

"I wish I was as clever as you, Mervin," she said, and grinned again.

Silly little thing . . .

And now back to the present. Time travel! Your mind wanders. Back to this rocky shore. And the stone and the sword.

Hold it . . . hold it . . .

I think . . .

Yes.

This looks like the one.

A slight young lad, not swaggering at all, but strolling up to the stone as if he's certain of his fortune. Ragged clothes, but that's not a problem, that's not a problem, we can do something about those later.

People are moving aside. It's uncanny. You can see Des-tiny unfolding, like a deck-chair.

Can't see much under the hood. It's one of those big floppy ones the peasants wear, but he's looking directly at me.

I wonder if he suspects? I wonder if he's real?

I wonder where he's been hiding all these years?

Well, never mind that now. Got to seize the moment. Shift my weight slightly, so my foot comes off the buried switch, cutting the current to the rock.

Good lord, he's not even making an effort. And up comes the sword, sweet as you like.

And everyone's cheering, and he's waving the thing in the air, and the sun's coming out and catching it in a way that even I couldn't arrange. *Ting.*

And it's done. They'll have to stop squabbling now. They've got their king and no one can argue with it, because they've all seen the miracle. Bright new future, etc, etc.

And, of course, he'll need some good advice from someone just like me.

And now he throws back his hood, and . . . *she* lets her blonde hair fall out, and the crowd goes ice-quiet.

We're not talking damsels here. She's smiling like a tiger, and looks as though she could do considerable damage with that sword.

I think the word I'm looking for is *imperious.*

She's daring them to protest, and they can't.

They've seen the miracle.

And she doesn't look like the kind of person who needs advice. She looks far too intelligent for my liking. She still looks like I first saw her at Ector's, with that bright stare that sees right into a man's soul. God help the little kings who don't come to heel right *now.*

I glance at Nimue. She's smiling an innocent little smile to herself.

I can't remember. She'd said "child," I can remember that, but did she ever actually say "son"?

I thought I was controlling the myth, but maybe I was just one of the players.

I bend down to Nimue's ear.

"Just out of interest," I say, "what is her name? Didn't catch it the first time."

"Ursula," she says, still smiling.

Ah. From the Latin for *bear*. I might have guessed.

Oh, well. Nothing for it. I suppose I'd better see if I can find enough decent seasoned timber for a Round Table, although for the life of me I can't guess who's going to sit around it. Not just a lot of thick-headed knights in tin trousers, that's for sure.

If I hadn't meddled she'd never have had a chance, and what chance does she have anyway? What *chance*?

I've looked into her eyes as she stared into mine. I can see the future.

I wonder how long it's going to be before we discover America?

Gwennhwyfar daughter of Cywryd Gwent, and Gwenhwyfar daughter of Gwythyr son of Griediawl, and Gwenhyfar daughter of Gogran the Giant

from "The Triad on the Three Great Queens of Arthur's Court," *Trioedd Yns Prydein—* *Triads of the Island of Britain*

Gwenhwyfar

Lynne Pledger

The two slaughtered calves hung in the doorway of the great barn. A sudden gust twirled them on the ends of their ropes.

Something within Gwenhwyfar quickened with the wind. Every autumn at the change in the weather, she felt that something extraordinary was about to happen. "But nothing extraordinary has happened for years," she reminded herself. "Not since I came to Wilbury."

"*Noli movere tauri*," said Urdick, thrusting his arms in front of Gwenhwyfar and the Abbess to steady the calf carcasses. The young man's splattered sleeves were rolled above his elbows; his forearms were white and smelled of soap. Gwenhwyfar lowered her eyes.

"*Nolite movere*," said the Abbess, correcting the cowherd's Latin. She drew herself up to her full height. "If you joined the Order you would have more time for study." Though Gwenhwyfar, at fifteen, was taller than the Abbess, the older woman always *seemed* taller, and now, in the slanted afternoon light, the nun looked ethereal.

But Urdick was looking out the barn door to the fields beyond. "I like working outside," he said.

Gwenhwyfar thought the Abbess stiffened slightly. No, she must have imagined it, because the nun replied smoothly, "You could continue to work outside. All the monks and nuns here at Wilbury do manual work when they're not studying—or praying, of course."

"I like working outside," Urdick repeated, as though the head of the great monastery hadn't spoken at all. Gwenhwyfar caught her breath.

But the nun's tone was suddenly pliant. "What a pity— you're a natural scholar." Though she had begun to examine the calf carcasses, she was watching Urdick out of the corner of her eye. "The way you've mastered Latin . . ."

"My Latin is better than his," Gwenhwyfar thought, heat rising to her face. She looked at the ground. The Abbess never fussed over her this way—not even when she announced her plans to take her vows.

"Who knows," the nun was saying to Urdick, "you could be a bishop someday!" Then, with an emphasis that made Gwenhwyfar look up again, she added, "People do go on from Wilbury. . . ."

"I like it here," was all Urdick had to say. Gwenhwyfar found herself nodding in agreement. Why would anyone want to leave Wilbury? But then the Abbess pursed her lips, and the girl knew the subject was closed. Urdick had lost his chance.

He turned one of the carcasses so that the two women could see the innards.

It was the little bull that had been born in the woods, his dam killed by a boar. Gwenhwyfar had found the newborn and carried him, trembling against her chest, all the way back to the barn. He'd sucked gratefully on her finger as she lowered his muzzle into warm milk.

Now the Abbess cleared her throat. Urdick and the Abbess were looking at Gwenhwyfar. Oh—were they waiting for *her* to make the decision? Flushing, she stood a little straighter. Of course! Who else at Wilbury knew as much about matters of the dairy?

She needed a calf's stomach for making cheese. A good one, that would yield enough rennet to turn their milk to curd through several seasons of cheese-making. She looked from one carcass to the other. The larger one was tinged with gray; a lingering sickness had corrupted the flesh. "I'll have the stomach from the smaller one." She indicated the little bull with a regal sweep of her arm.

Living with the nuns, she tended to forget she was the daughter of a king.

Her parents were long dead of a fever, and her father's kingdom—never large—had been divided by the neighboring kings, who had taken her in the back of a cart and left her at the monastery for lack of any better place. Her royal blood counted for nothing at Wilbury. They had put her to work in the dairy, where she found, to her surprise, that the round of exacting tasks suited her. For a time she had clung to her memories, then one by one she had laid them away, like tapestries too fine to be of any use.

"You'll not want the other maw as well?" Urdick prompted gently, with a nod at the larger carcass.

"No," Gwenhwyfar snapped, though there was no reason to be irritable—Urdick was well-meaning.

"It's not fit for rennet," she explained. "It would taint the milk." The carcass wasn't fit for veal either, but she hesitated to say so. The Abbess would be marketing it. Gwenhwyfar knew nothing of trade. On the other hand, she did know off-color veal. "The hide, the hooves, and the tallow are all that should be saved," she said, her voice sounding louder than she intended. For a moment she regretted her boldness.

Urdick looked at the Abbess. The nun acknowledged Gwenhwyfar's expertise with a nod.

The girl lowered her eyes, hoping to conceal her pride. The Abbess frowned on pride; Gwenhwyfar's abilities were gifts from God. "The Abbess doesn't seem displeased about losing the sale of the veal," the girl thought.

Urdick cut the stomach from the healthy carcass and solemnly handed it to Gwenhwyfar. "Like a knight of the Round Table presenting his lady with an embroidered pocket," she said to herself with a smile as she dropped the maw into the bucket. In fact, Urdick, with his mild manner and spattered clothes, was not at all like King Arthur's knights. She knew; in recent months the Abbess had entertained several delegations from the High King, and more than once she had called Gwenhwyfar into their presence, for some reason that was never made clear.

Gwenhwyfar

Now the Abbess dismissed her with a distracted nod. The nun's green eyes were cool and distant, like the sea. Already something else was on her mind, Gwenhwyfar realized. She walked slowly toward the dairy, the bucket knocking against her leg.

The wind whipped her cloak, and she shivered, not entirely from the chill. "The weather always changes after harvest, and nothing ever happens . . ." she reassured herself, as she bowed her head before the wind.

Entering the dairy, she was at once cheered by the glow from the firepit and the familiar clutter of buckets and basins. There was still the cream to be skimmed, so she made quick work of cleaning the maw, dropped it into a kettle of brine, and picked up a cream pot and skimmer. Then, turning from the brightness of the fire, she paused in the doorway of the milkroom, as though entering a church.

The inner room of the dairy had a high ceiling and stone floor, left from the days when a Roman fortress occupied the site. It was dark and cool and smelled of ripening cheese. The twelve round basins of milk from last night's milking were evenly spaced along the central table like pale moons. She stepped up to the first one and slid the skimmer around its inside edge, folding the sheet of cream over and over on itself. Then she scooped it from the bluish milk, dropped it—*splat*—into the pot, and went on to the next basin.

Caught up in the rhythm of the work, she sang a half-remembered song:

> *The lady's at the spindle, thy lord is in the mews,*
> *Pick a pasty, pick a sweet,*

67

Thy babe is far too young to choose.
Jesses tangle, spindle dangle,
Far too young——

There was a noise from the front room. It was early for the novices to be coming for the milk buckets; she looked over her shoulder. In the doorway was a dark-robed figure outlined by the firelight. The Abbess.

Normally the nun would be at prayer at this hour. Apprehensive and yet vaguely hopeful, Gwenhwyfar held her breath. But the older woman said nothing, so the girl turned to her basins again. Still the nun remained in the doorway, casting her shadow over the table. Unable to see the work, Gwenhwyfar looked back at her uncertainly.

Just then the Abbess lifted the hem of her gown to step onto the stone floor, and the girl glimpsed a linen tunic beneath the dark wool. Abruptly she looked away.

Linen! The Order must be thriving for the Abbess to be buying imported cloth. When Gwenhwyfar had come to live there as a child, the monastery was newly founded, and the monks and nuns as lean as the odd, red cattle they'd brought with them. But the cows had thrived on the scant grass and browse of the hilltop site; now Wilbury was profiting at trade.

And now that the monastery was well-established, Gwenhwyfar reflected, she was well-established too. There was no telling what position she might be given when she took her vows. Someday she'd like to be Cellaress, responsible for provisions for the entire estate, working closely with the Abbess. Why, someday she might even be——

"White as curd, what little there is," said the nun, who had glided to her side and was peering into the cream pot.

"Yes, it's that time of year." Gwenhwyfar smiled as she picked up the skimmer again. "In June when the grass is lush, the cream is yellow, and so thick I can lift it off the milk like a piece of leather." The Abbess didn't seem to be listening, so she simply added, "By Christmas we'll have the last of the milk."

"No," the older woman corrected. "This year we'll milk the cows until they calve again in the spring."

"But in winter, it's all they can do to keep the meat on their bones, and if—" Gwenhwyfar bit off her protest.

"They'll keep giving milk for as long as we keep milking them," the Abbess went on smoothly. "There's plenty of food in the woods, and if they're hungry they'll find it."

The girl nodded. "They're clever that way, where other cattle would starve, but—"

"And by spring sweet butter will be worth its weight in gold."

There was no denying that. Gwenhwyfar finished the skimming and turned to the cheeses, which were arranged on shelves according to when they were pressed. But as she worked down the line of them, lifting, wiping, and turning each one, she couldn't help worrying about the cows being milked all year until they calved—only to be milked for another year, and then to calve again.

Was this what the Abbess had come to tell her?

The nun was strolling the length of the far wall, her white fingers trailing over the casks of butter and salt. Pausing beside a stack of new tubs, she asked, "Have these been inventoried?"

Though the Abbess had never questioned her record-keeping, the girl replied evenly, "Yes, everything is current."

"And the butter is all salted away?"

"Well, not all—" Gwenhwyfar began.

But the Abbess was walking toward the door, murmuring, "And the novices are thoroughly trained in every aspect of the work."

Then, almost as an afterthought, she turned to Gwenhwyfar. "A delegation from the High King will be arriving tonight. They'll be leaving again at daybreak for Camelot, and you will be leaving with them . . ." For a moment Gwenhwyfar thought she was being sent away because she hadn't salted all the butter. But the Abbess continued, ". . . to become King Arthur's new queen."

"King Arthur's new queen?" the girl repeated.

"Yes." The Abbess squared her shoulders. "A Christian queen over all of Britain." She went on about arrangements for the marriage.

Gwenhwyfar stood perfectly still as though the words might pass by without touching her. Then she recalled the recent flurry of delegations from the king, the appraising stares of his men . . . and understanding struck her like a blow. "My life is here!" she gasped. "I'm going to take my vows—"

The Abbess arched her eyebrows. Turning from the girl she asked, "Even if it's God's will that you serve Him and all of Britain as King Arthur's queen?"

"They'll be leaving again at daybreak for Camelot, and you will be leaving with them ..."

"But my work . . ." Gwenhwyfar waved her arm to take in the room. "I love . . ." Then she shook her head from side to side. "There must be other young women of royal blood—women who could bring wealth to the marriage—dowerlands—"

The Abbess said curtly, "None with your impeccable virtue and lineage." She paused. "And none as able or learned."

Gwenhwyfar was beginning another protest but at the unaccustomed praise from the nun she stopped. Her skin tingled pleasantly with sudden warmth, as if she'd come from the shadows into the sun.

The nun was saying, "There's your command of Latin . . ."

The girl flushed and lowered her eyes. She had done some transcribing in the monastery's scriptorium; she wondered if the Abbess had mentioned this to the king's representatives. She imagined them telling the king, and the king being impressed.

"Your years at Wilbury have prepared you well for your new responsibilities," the Abbess went on. "And you will be following a proud tradition." She spoke of powerful British queens who brought their influence to bear on church and kingdom. Her eyes were sparkling, and she was smiling broadly. Smiling at Gwenhwyfar.

Suddenly the girl was so lighthearted she was dizzy. The rest of the interview went by in a blur.

Then it was over, and she'd forgotten to ask how long ago the queen had passed away. She had heard that the middle-aged sovereign was of a melancholic humor, but she hadn't heard that the queen had died.

That night, long after she should have been asleep, Gwenhwyfar sat wide-eyed on her bed in the front room of the dairy, fingering her mother's gold necklace. She had planned to relinquish it to the Order when she took her vows. Now it would be her parting gift to the Abbess. It would say what Gwenhwyfar could not.

The necklace was all she had of her life before coming to Wilbury. On Gwenhwyfar's ninth birthday her mother had summoned a servant to remove her necklace and give it to her daughter. Her father had waved the maid away and waited on his wife himself, gently moving her hair to one side to find the clasp. Gwenhwyfar could still see her mother's dark fall of hair, the slope of her shoulder . . . but for some reason, she could not remember her face.

In the months following the death of her parents, she had longed to see her mother's face again—even in her sleep. One night she had dreamed she was spinning in the tower of her father's castle and heard her mother talking in the room below. Savoring the sweetness of the sound, she had slowly descended the stairs. But she had awakened before reaching the bottom.

That had been five years ago.

Now she put the necklace back into its doeskin bag, and lay back on her mat. Once again the thought of leaving Wilbury brought a lump to her throat. She took a deep breath, then slowly let it out. She wanted to remember the mingled smells of the room. Closing her eyes, she tried to fix them in her mind one by one: the musty cow-smell that clung to her clothes, the pungent smell of the scouring herbs, the sour milk-smell . . . she was really very tired . . . the wet-wooden-bucket-smell . . . the cooking smells drifting up into the tower . . .

She was spinning in the tower of her father's castle. Suddenly she heard her mother talking in the room below. The sound was like a caress. But she told herself, "My mother is dead; she cannot be there." Then, from the bottom of the stairwell, in a voice clear and true, her mother called to her—"Gwenhwyfar!"—and a wild hope seized the girl. Down the winding stairway she ran, weeping and stumbling, down, down, until finally she reached the bottom. Turning, she looked into the cool green eyes of the Abbess.

The next day never actually dawned; the sky simply lightened to gray. The wind whipped Gwenhwyfar's new cloak—a present from the king—causing the horses of the royal delegation to stamp and whinny as Urdick readied them for the journey to Camelot.

The Abbess was at prayer and could not be there to see her off, so Gwenhwyfar had left the necklace with the Cellaress. "The Abbess might have it by now," the girl thought, as she and the rest of the party mounted. Her gaze went from one faceless window of the Abbey to the next.

Even the paddock by the refectory was empty. She was sorry not to see the cattle once more; she would have liked to say goodbye.

Urdick, who was checking and rechecking her stirrups, explained, "The Abbess is keeping the cattle in the barn until the king's men have gone." The girl nodded, remembering a time when Wilbury's sheep had been requisitioned to feed the king's foot-soldiers as they passed through the area. When Urdick added, "The Abbess wouldn't risk losing her valuable cows to the king," Gwenhwyfar wondered at his bitter tone.

The king had not come for her himself, but besides the cloak and her saddle horse, he had sent a serving woman who, by her own account, had been caring for young queens all her life.

To cover her nervousness, Gwenhwyfar admired the bronze-studded saddles and colored saddle blankets of the king's delegation, saying to her serving woman, "If the horses at Camelot dress so fine, I can't imagine what the ladies wear!" Then she frowned; it still troubled her that she brought no dowry to the marriage. She expressed her concern to her companion.

The serving woman shook her head. "Don't you be worryin' about that. The way everybody figures it, it's perfect— you an orphan an' all. That way, if it don't . . . I mean, if you can't . . ." She reddened and looked away.

Gwenhwyfar's skin prickled.

Everything had happened so fast. There was something she must know. "The queen . . . I mean, the . . . my Lord's first wife . . ."

The servant nodded. "Queen Gwenhwyfar? She was a 'Gwenhwyfar' too, you know."

The girl blurted, "What happened to her?"

The older woman's eyes widened. "The way I figured it, everyone knew. . . ." Then she added hurriedly, "But don't you be worryin'. You'll bear him a son."

The horses began to move out of the yard.

The girl gripped the pommel of her saddle. "A son?" she said, her voice unnaturally high.

"A son—an heir to the throne." The woman reached over and patted Gwenhwyfar's knee. "A big, strapping girl like yourself will bear sons—likely one every year! And so rosy and bloomin' like you are, the king will be pleased enough."

Gwenhwyfar twisted around in the saddle. They were just past the dairy. . . .

The serving woman was going on about her attributes. "—sweet breath; not a tooth missing in your mouth—or so she said."

Slowly Gwenhwyfar turned to look at the older woman. "Who said?" she whispered.

"—smooth skin—"

"*Who* said?" Suddenly her voice was shrill.

Her servant said immediately, "Why, the Abbess."

The Abbess? *Not a tooth missing in her mouth.* That's what the Abbess had said of her?

Gwenhwyfar was numb. She couldn't seem to move her arms and legs. She stared at the hands in her lap; resting against the fine cloth of the cloak, they already seemed like the hands of a stranger. Fingers thickened from milking. Nails worn square and smooth. Capable hands.

The serving woman was saying, "The way I figure it—"

A gust of wind rolled a bucket across the barnyard where just yesterday Gwenhwyfar had stood with Urdick and the Abbess.

"—a healthy girl like yourself is as fit as any to be queen."

The carcass of a calf, still hanging in the doorway of the barn, twirled at the end of a rope.

Just then Arthur saw that in the center of the lake the surface was broken by an arm, clothed in white samite, and that the hand grasped a finely jeweled sword and scabbard.

"That is the magic sword Excalibur," said Merlin, "and it will be given to you by the Lady of the Lake. . . ."

from *Le Morte d' Arthur* by
Sir Thomas Malory

Excalibur

Anne E. Crompton

Lady's Wood lied in the midst of Tall Country. Wise Tall Ones stay away from Lady's Wood. Only one Tall man in the world has ever entered our Wood, or looked upon our Lake. And some say that he is a changeling, one of Us, left in a Tall cradle at birth.

Sentinels watch Tall Country day and night from high trees on the edge of Lady's Wood. This morning some of us girls are sentinels. I perch high in an ancient oak, wrapped in my green cloak. With that and my nut-brown skin, I am invisible.

The other sentinels talk in our code of bird-calls and squirrel chatter. I am silent. I think, brood, worry about my Great Fault, and my smaller fault. These two faults cause much comment. We Forest Folk are severe with faults.

A willow warbler calls, "Children hoeing peas!"

I know those children, though they have never glimpsed me. They leave food for us at a standing stone in Sir Ektor's fields; milk, peas, bread. Each child wears a small iron charm to protect him from us. But we wish them no harm. The smallest one, half my age, is my size.

A mistle thrush chirps, "Knights riding!"

Here they come over the fields, three dark figures on three huge, dark horses.

A squirrel scolds, "Keep to the road, Knights! You're trampling good barley."

If they were visitors on their way to Sir Ektor, they would keep to the road. If they were honest knights they would carry a standard. I whistle, "Brigands! Those are brigands!"

A chaffinch reminds me sweetly, "No matter to us."

Right. What the Tall Ones do to each other in their own world is no matter to us, so long as they stay out of our Wood.

Our Wood is holy, the Lake at its center is holy, the secret Treasure under the Lake is holy beyond measure. Our mission is to guard Wood, Lake and Treasure. We warn the Tall Ones away with red-dyed mistletoe, with bushes cut to look like monsters, with feather-crowned skeletons. Tall Ones who pass these warnings fall into pits, or are snatched high in noose-traps. Wise Tall Ones stay away from Lady's Wood. Even the serf children hoeing peas know that.

Nearer the brigands ride. The children stop hoeing to watch them.

Sunlight glints on the brigands' light armor, on their helmets. The one in front lowers his visor and spurs his lumbering horse.

The children drop their hoes and run for a copse between two fields.

The brigands gallop into the peas.

I hear the cry as the smallest, slowest child dodges flying hooves.

I hear the shout as the first rider topples off his horse.

The brigand struggles up, keeping his horse between himself and the copse. An arrow trembles in his shoulder.

His companions leap off their horses, draw swords, run toward the copse.

A tall boy bursts out of the copse on our side, running for Lady's Wood.

We all know him. He is Sir Ektor's son. Hunting hares in Sir Ektor's fields, his brothers call him "Arthur." I have seen him run before now, empty quiver bouncing, yellow hair streaming. Never have I seen him run faster than now, after shooting the brigand.

The brigands halloo in the copse. They see him. The hunt is on.

My toes touch ground. I must have moved when the child cried out. I must have climbed down the oak, unknowing.

Silently, swiftly, I move through fern to intercept Arthur. My careful step breaks no twig. I move bent over, green cloak slung around me like a shadow.

Gods, I am unarmed! I left my spear under the oak. This carelessness is my small fault. I think I am the only girl of the Forest Folk who could climb down an oak unknowing, or leave her spear behind!

What should I do now? Nothing. Stop. Let Sir Ektor's Arthur take care of himself.

81

What will I do? I don't know.

Here is the trail Arthur will follow. I crouch and throw my green cloak around me.

Birds, squirrels, mice chatter and squeak. "What are you doing?" they ask. "You are a sentinel, go back to your tree! We can handle this."

I mouse-squeak, "This one is mine! Leave him to me!" I don't know why.

Here comes Arthur. Feet thud, bright hair flops, blue eyes gleam. As he bounds past, I grab his ankle.

I yank him down off the trail, lie beside him, throw my cloak over both of us.

He gasps and stinks. Twice my size, he smells of smoke, ale, beef. Gods, he might even have cursed iron on him, a knife, perhaps! I want to throw up.

Thud, pant, dirty word. Giant boots pause in front of us. A huge male voice roars, "Vanished!"

"Can't go far," rasps a second voice. "This is Forest Folk country."

"What!"

"You saw the red mistletoe."

"Not me, I just saw him. Let's get out of here!"

"Not so fast, friend. You want to report we trailed and lost him?"

"No need to report."

"Look, we've come a way to slit this kid's throat. There's gold in it."

"Aye!" Greed thickens the first voice. "Gold, just to kill a boy!" The brigand lowers his voice to a whisper like wild, sweeping rain. "And I've heard the Forest Folk guard gold in their hideouts!"

We have no gold under Lady's Lake. We have a Treasure worth far more than gold, and through my Fault these stinking brigands may find it. For this I will answer to the Lady!

The brigands' coarse voices hurt my ears. Our men are soft-spoken. Our men have eyes, ears and noses. They would have found Arthur and me by now.

The second brigand says, "I've heard wise men stay away from the Forest Folk. We'll just wipe out this Arthur kid and go. Halloo!" He shouts to all of the silent, listening Lady's Wood. "We don't want none of your gold, Folks! We just want Sir Ektor's boy, that's all. No business of yours, Folks. No gold!"

The two men tramp past us, to the bend of the trail. Around the bend they will crash into a hidden pit.

Arthur moves.

He lifts the cloak up to look after them. The cloak drags leaves, snaps a stick.

"Hoy!" A brigand swings round. "Halloo, there he is!"

We are up and running. My cloak, like my spear, lies abandoned.

I lead Arthur down trails he cannot see. He runs stooped under branch and thorn, through clearings where astonished Folk watch by their grass huts. Behind him the brigands roar like hounds on a stag's trail. Arthur is like a young stag with glossy coat and budding antlers, strong, swift, frightened. We Forest Folk have been known to turn a hunt before now. Yet the Folk stare at me, amazed and angry.

Shall I hide Arthur up a leafy tree? The brigands are too close for that.

Shall I lead them into a pit? Arthur might fall in first.

Close ahead lies safety. It is holy, secret, forbidden. But my Great Fault has turned this hunt, and now I must end it.

I bound lightly across the first entrance to safety, a hidden burrow. Arthur could never squeeze in there. He probably thinks it's a rabbit hole.

The next entrance, a hollow beech, would be obvious even to the brigands. We pound past it and burst out of the woods into wide summer light.

Below us sparkles Lady's Lake. Only one Tall man in the world has ever stood on this cliff and looked out over Lady's Lake. Only one Tall man till now.

We pause but a moment on the cliff. Behind us branches swish, heavy boots tread.

I grab Arthur's large, hot fingers. We jump.

Vines snake up and down the cliff, screening ledge and crevice. We land on a hidden ledge, I pull Arthur back into a hidden crevice. I push him back, back, where the brigands will not hear him gasp. I listen at the vine.

The brigands stand above us, two Tall Men, greedy and cruel, looking over Lady's Lake. For this I will answer to the Lady.

One says, "Vanished again."

"Not swimming. If he jumped he's done for. Want to check?"

"I've had enough of this place. Feels like we're watched."

"We are, friend, we are! Wise men stay away from here."

"Let's go."

They can try.

Holding Arthur's fingers I lead him down the crevice into the secret cave, into darkness. I forget how tall he is. After he runs head-on into rock, he crawls. Down we go, around boulders, under lowering ceilings. Toward the end I have to crawl myself. Arthur worm-wriggles.

Soft light glimmers around a corner. We lie at the cave entrance, panting.

An everlasting fire burns in Lady's Cave under the Lake. The Old Ones tend it, those who can no longer run and climb. Three Old Ones sit around it now, watching us. Low firelight gleams on white hair and beards, beads and shells.

Arthur and I scramble up.

Rowan, the oldest, says, "Come where we can see you."

I straighten my tunic, smooth my hair. Slowly, with dignity, I lead Arthur to the fire.

Rowan says to him, "You are tall, young man." His old eyes sharpen. *"You are a Tall young man."*

Arthur booms, "I can't help that, Sir." His voice echoes from cave wall to cave wall, far beyond the firelight.

I try to explain. "Rowan, I led him here. Brigands hunted him."

"Indeed?" Rowan marvels at me. "And what was that to you?"

"I . . . don't know."

"That was your Great Fault, girl. And why could you not stop the brigands yourself, before they ever entered our Wood?"

"I . . . left my spear behind."

85

"That was your second fault. Girl, you are faulty!"

Rowan turns to Arthur. "Tall young man, know that this place is holy. Secret. Forbidden."

Arthur says quickly, "I will take an oath to keep this secret. I will swear by . . ." He looks around for something the Tall Ones swear by.

"Hah!" says Rowan.

"Hah!" say the other Old Ones. And they laugh.

I fear their laughter, that cold, determined victory laughter.

Arthur hears death in that laughter. He grasps the knife at his belt.

"No need to swear," a male voice says softly, from darkness.

Merlin Magician steps into light. Merlin is not very Tall, and we consider him ours. Some say he was a changeling, left in a Tall cradle at birth. He is old now, white-haired, slightly stooped. Yet he moves gracefully, smiling in his beard.

Merlin travels the world, from kingdom to kingdom, forest to forest. He brings news, he recalls the past and foretells the future. So I am not surprised that Arthur knows him.

A small cry of relief escapes Arthur. He lifts his hand from his iron knife.

A second figure steps soundlessly into the firelight.

Cloaked, the Lady is a shadow. At Merlin's side she drops her cloak and shines. Bright flowers crown her long dark hair. Pearls and shells and crystals sparkle up and down her robe. The gems catch firelight like fire. In her arms the Lady carries a long, slender package wrapped in brown wool.

In her arms the Lady carries a long, slender package wrapped in brown wool.

"No need to swear, Arthur," Merlin says. "My Forgetful Cup can wipe all memory of this place and time from your mind."

"Ah." Arthur sighs.

"But now, while you are here," Merlin adds, "know who you are."

To my surprise Arthur smiles at that. "I've always wondered," he says. "I know Sir Ektor is not my father." He is not? "When I watch clouds pass, or sunlight on water, I feel who I am. But I cannot name myself."

Merlin says gently, "In this moment, which you will forget utterly, I will name you. You are Arthur, son of Pendragon, High King to be."

Arthur stares into Merlin's eyes as though tranced. "Yes," he murmurs. "That is what I knew."

A hand rests on my arm. I glance down at rings and bracelets. The glowing Lady touches me.

Her voice laps like water. "Hold out your arms."

She places that which she carries across my arms.

"Hold the Treasure."

It is long, hard and heavy. It burns my arms through the wool wrap.

I whisper, "Iron!"

"Do not be afraid."

The Lady lifts away the wrap.

Light leaps from Excalibur's hilt. The Lady draws away the richly embroidered scabbard, and the naked sword shines like a torch, lighting the cavern even to the far, damp walls. I hold the Treasure stiffly, swaying under its weight.

The Lady turns to Arthur.

"Long ago," she tells him, "the sword Excalibur was wielded by a Tall king we trusted. While he reigned, Forest Folk and Tall Ones were friends.

"Since his day we have kept Excalibur under our Lake. It is our Treasure, and our hope. Prophets have told us another king we trust will reign, and Forest Folk and Tall Ones will again enjoy friendship, for a time."

To me she says, "Give Excalibur to Arthur."

I look up into Arthur's face, across the gleaming sword. His is a strong, honest young face. Arthur shot the brigand to save the serf child. He will fight for right. I see that in his steady blue eyes. Swaying, I lift Excalibur toward him.

Arthur's large, hot hand grasps the hilt. He holds Excalibur high. The cavern reflects Excalibur's light like sunlight.

Merlin says, "When the time comes, the Lady of the Lake will give you Excalibur."

Dreamily, Arthur murmurs, "I will accept it."

"And when the time comes she will take it back."

"I will give it back."

The Lady takes Excalibur from Arthur. She slips it into its scabbard. As Excalibur slides into its scabbard, light slips into shadow. The far cavern walls hide again in darkness.

"Come now," Merlin tells Arthur. "You can drink my Forgetful Cup at the Wood's edge and go home."

But Arthur pauses to bow to me. "I thank you, Lady," he says. Then he goes, vanishing with Merlin Magician into the dark.

And now. Now I face the Lady. Now I answer for all that has happened, for my Great Fault and my small fault.

I have heard tales of faulty Folk turned into toads, or locked in hollow trees. I face the Lady.

She smiles. She says, "When the time comes, you will give Excalibur to Arthur."

"I?" But Merlin said the Lady of the Lake would do that.

"For a time, a new spirit will live in the land. During Arthur's reign Forest Folk and Tall Ones will be at peace, and the Tall Ones will be friends among themselves.

"But this state cannot last for long. The Forest Folk will hide again in secret retreats. Arthur's Peace will remain only as a vision of peace, a legend, remembered forever. When his reign ends you will take Excalibur back from Arthur."

"I? But Lady, Merlin Magician said—"

"We Forest Folk are wise, but most of us lack Heart."

Heart! Heart is my Great Fault! All my life I have been scolded and warned because I have Heart.

"The next Lady of the Lake will have to deal closely with the Tall Ones. To understand them, she will need Heart. A small carelessness, too, will help make her seem familiar to the Tall Ones. New times need new virtues," says the Lady. "You have Heart, and you have this small carelessness. You, the next Lady of the Lake, will deal with Arthur."

She smiles and wraps herself in her cloak. Now the only light flickers from the everlasting fire. The shadowy Lady and shrouded Excalibur vanish into darkness. The three Old Ones still sit in firelight, looking up at me.

Out in the sunlight, Arthur is drinking from Merlin's Forgetful Cup.

It may be that he has already forgotten us, the Cave, and

even Excalibur. Or he may tell Merlin about his strange dream as they walk home together to Sir Ektor's castle.

When we meet again, Arthur will not know me.

But I will know Arthur. Forgetfulness is not for me. Cold wisdom and watchfulness will always be for me. I may have Heart, but the gods know well that I am of the Folk.

Before Geraint, the enemy's scourage,
I saw white horses, tensed, red . . .
In Llongborth I saw spurs
And men who did not flinch from
   spears . . .
In Llongborth I saw Arthur's
Heroes who cut from steel.
The Emperor, ruler of our labour. . . .
Under the thigh of Geraint swift chargers,
Long their legs, wheat their fodder,
Red, swooping like milk-white eagles . . .

from *The Black Book of Camarthen,*
                    twelfth century

Black Horses for a King

Anne McCaffrey

By now, I was some used to crossing the Narrow Sea, but to have to tend to six grown men who were not, made me as ill as they. And made me, once again, the butt for jokes from my uncle's crew.

"Galwyn's feeding the fishes again," the mate called as I emptied the odorous bucket overboard. I ignored him, rinsing the bucket in the strong waves that were following us from Isca Dumnorium. It had taken me a while to learn not to rise to his lures: he'd leave off his taunts sooner. "Have ye no seablood in ye at all? Ye're no use in the rigging, little use on deck and ye can't even keep b'low decks clean."

I was hauling the bucket up, had it nearly to the rail when a particularly hungry wave caught and filled it. The line pulled burningly through my hands. I only managed to belay it on a pin and thus not lose it entirely. The mate roared with laughter, encouraging the other men of his watch to join him, at my unhandiness.

"Galwyn, I'd want proof that y'are indeed Gralior's nephew if I'd one like ye on any ship of mine."

The bucket forgotten, I whirled on him for that insult to my mother.

"Ah, lad, we've sore need of the bucket below," said a deep voice in my ear. A hand caught my shoulder with a powerful shake to gain my attention and curb my intent. "Such taunts are the currency of the petty," our noble passenger continued for my ear alone. "Treat them with the contempt they deserve." Then he went on in a tone meant to carry, "I tried the salted beef as you suggested, and it has succeeded in settling my belly. For which I'm obliged to you. I'll have another plate for my Companions."

I could not recall the man's name, a Roman one for all he was supposed to be as much a Briton as the rest of us. My uncle had treated him with more respect, even reverence, than he accorded most men, fare-paying passengers or not. So I was quite as willing to obey this Briton Lord, this Comes, without quibble, and ease his Companions' distress in any way I could. I hauled up the bucket, which he took below with him. Then I got more salt beef from the barrel before I followed him back down into the space assigned the passengers.

Warriors they might be, but on the sea and three days from land, they were in woeful condition: two were green under their weathered skins as they lay defeated by the roll and heave of the deck beneath them. I did not laugh, all too familiar with their malaise. They were big men, strong of arm and thew, with calloused hands and arms scarred by swordplay. They'd swords in their baggage and oiled leather jerkins well studded with nails. Big men in search of big horses to carry them into battle against the Saxons. That much I had gleaned from snatches of their conversation before the seasickness robbed them of talk and dignity.

"Come now, Flavian, you see me revived," the war chief cajoled. Flavian, one of the six, merely moaned as the salt beef was dangled in front of his face and gestured urgently to me to bring the bucket. There could be nothing now but bile in the man's stomach, if that, for he had drunk no more than a sip or two of water. "Bericus, will you not try the salt beef, young Galwyn's magic cure?" The second man at arms closed his eyes and slapped a great fist across his nose and mouth. "Come now, Companions, we are all but there, are we not, young Galwyn?"

I was mortified that he had remembered my name when I could not recall his, and started to duck my head away from his smiling face. Now I was caught by the brilliant blue of his eyes and held by an indefinable link which made of me, in that one moment, his fervent adherent. Ah, if only my uncle would award me such a glance, I could have found my apprenticeship far easier to bear.

"Aye, sir," I said with an encouraging smile for the low-laid Bericus, "we'll make port soon and that's the truth!" For landfall was indeed nigh. I'd seen the smudge on the horizon when I'd emptied the bucket, though the mate's taunt had driven the fact out of my mind. "We should be up the river to Burtigala by dusk. Solid, dry land."

"Artos, if the rest of this mad scheme of yours is as perilous as this . . ." Bericus said in a petulant growl.

"Come now, *amici,*" their leader said cheerfully, "this very evening I shall see you served meat, fowl, fish, whatever viand you wish . . ." Each suggestion brought a groan from Bericus, and Flavian tossed his soiled mantle over his head in repudiation.

"We're in the river now, Lord," I said to the Comes Britannorium Artos, for his full name came back to me now. Even if the others did not, I could feel the difference in the ship's motion. "If you'd come up on deck now, sirs, you'll not find the motion so distressing as lying athwart it down here."

Lord Artos flashed me a grin and, hauling the reluctant Bericus to his feet, said: "That's a good thought, lad. Come, clear your head of the sick miasma. Fresh air is what you need now to set you right." He gestured for me to help Flavian as he went to rouse the rest of his Companions.

They staggered, almost falling back down the ladder at the impact of the fresh air. One and all, they reeled toward the deck, with me hard put to get them to the leeward rail lest they find their own spew whipped back into their faces.

"Look at the land," I suggested. "Not the sea nor the deck. The land won't move."

"If it does, I shall never be the same," Bericus muttered, with a dark glance toward his leader who stood, feet braced, head back, his long tawny hair whipped back like a legion pennant. Bericus groaned. "And to think we've got to come back this same way!"

"It will not be as bad on the way back, sir," I said, to encourage him.

He raised his eyebrows, his pale eyes bright in amazement. "Nay, it'll be worse for we'll have the bloody horses to tend . . . on that!" He gestured behind him at the following seas. "Flavian, d'you know? Can horses get seasick?"

"I'll be sure to purchase only those guaranteed to have sealegs," the Comes said with a wink to me.

I looked away lest any of the others misconstrue my expression. For this was August and the crossing had been reasonably calm. In a month or so, the autumn gales could start and those could be turbulent enough to empty the bellies of hardened seamen.

"Have you far to travel on land?" I asked.

"To the horse fair at Septimania," Lord Artos said negligently.

"Where might that be, Lord?"

His eyes twinkled approval at my question. "In the shadow of the Pyrenaei mountains, in Narbo Martius."

"That far, Lord?" I was aghast.

"To find that which I must have," and his voice altered, his eyes lost their focus, and his fists clenched above the railing, "to do what I must do . . ."

I felt a surge run up from my bowels at the stern purpose of his manner and experienced an errant desire to smooth his way however I could. Foolish of me who had so little to offer anyone, and yet this Britic war chief was a man above men.

97

He made me, an insignificant and inept apprentice, feel less a failure and more confident in his presence.

"And it is mine to do," he added, exhaling the tension of his own inner fervor. Then he smiled down at me, allowing me a small share of his certain goal.

"I need big strong mares and stallions to breed the war-horses we need to drive the Saxons out of our lands and back into the sea," he went on in a vibrant and compelling tone. "Horses powerful enough to carry warriors in full regalia, fast and far. For it is the swift, unexpected strike that will cause havoc among the Saxon forces, unaccustomed to cavalry in battle. Julius Caesar used the 'alauda,' his Germanic cavalry, to good effect. I shall take that page from the scroll of his accomplishments and protect Briton with *my* horsemen.

"If God is with us, the mares and stallions I need will be at that horse fair in Septimania, bred by the Goths from the same Libyan blood stock that the Romans used."

"Will not the Legions return, Lord, to help us?" I asked hopefully. I'd heard enough about their abilities to see them as the sure answer to those Saxon marauders, and the Irish war bands which occasionally attacked Isca Dumnorium.

Lord Artos gave me a kind smile. "No, lad, we cannot expect them. This we must do for ourselves. The horses are the key."

"*Do* horses get seasick?" Bericus asked pointedly, having listened quietly to the exchange.

"The Legions got theirs to Briton. Why can we not do the same?" the Comes asked with a wry grin.

"But how, Lord, will you transport them?" and I gestured

at the narrow hatch to the lower deck. Not even a shaggy Sorviodunum pony could pass through it.

"Ah, now that's the easy part," Artos said, rubbing his big, scarred hands together. "Cador and I worked that out." My eyes must have bulged at his casual reference to our Prince of Dumnonia, for he gave me another reassuring smile which somehow included me in such exalted company. "We lift the deck planks, settle the horses below in pens, well bedded on straw, and nail the planks back on. Simple, *sa?*"

I was not the only dubious listener but the Lord Artos seemed so sure and Prince Cador had the reputation of a formidably acute man.

"How big are the horses from Septimania?" I asked.

Artos put his forearm at a level with his eyes. "That height in the shoulder."

I could only stare at him in amazement. "Surely horses are not meant to grow that big?"

"Why ever not, Galwyn, when we have?" And Artos gestured to his Companions, all of whom towered above me, though I was considered the tall one of my kin.

Then my uncle came on deck, shouting orders to prepare the ship for her landing. The *Corellia* ran up the mouth of the broad Gallish river to the harbor at Burtigala as if eager to end her journey. I hoped that there would be a cargo for us to return with or my uncle's humor would be sour indeed. On this outbound trip, there had only been a load of bull-hides, though the seven passengers had been a godsend and made the sailing worthwhile.

I also hoped that there would be occasion for me to assist in obtaining a good cargo to confirm me in my uncle's good graces. I was still on probation in his employ. Certainly I was no sailor, but I was of use to him in port, to translate some of the barbarous trading dialects. It was for this fluency that my uncle tolerated my other shortcomings.

From childhood, I had been exposed to many foreign tongues. My father, Decitus Varianus, had been a Factor, an agent, and met folk from as far away as Egypt and Greece to the East and some of the roving Nordish folk from the North. An outgoing, curious child, I had picked up snitches and snatches of many languages—sometimes hardly knowing what I was saying but the facility remained and was improved upon by tutors in Greek and Latin, the Gaelic of our hill farmers, and indeed, whatever outlandish speech was spoken about me.

After we had safely tied up at the Roman pier, I hovered around Lord Artos and his Companions, helping them with their packs and gear. I was unwilling to leave their company. Well, *his* company. As I had hoped—since Lord Artos was so well acquainted with our Prince—my uncle bade me guide them to the best inn of the town and see them comfortably settled in case they should find themselves unable to understand the landlord's rough speech.

That night, as I lay on a straw pallet in the hold of the *Corellia,* still redolent of seasick odors, I thought of Comes Artos's quest. *Horses!* How much I missed our horses. Before my father had lost all his substance in two seasons of disastrous storms, we had had many fine beasts in our stables: I had had a mettlesome pony whom I had ridden as if we two were a single centaur. My father's sergeant at arms had grudgingly admitted that I was likely to make a competent horseman (praise indeed from that stern fellow). What time I had to spare from my lessons and duties as my father's heir had been spent in the stable. When my father had fallen upon his sword rather than face ignominious bankruptcy, my uncle—my mother's elder brother—had grudgingly taken me in. He and his family made a litany out of how much I owed him for his charity, taking the son of a failed man, a spoiled juvenile with but one skill with which I might earn a humble living.

I ought not even to think of horses: they brought back too many painful memories. But I could scarcely help myself. Fine big strong horses, to be ridden by fine big strong men! *Surely* they'd need a horseboy to assist them on their travels? *Surely* I could make myself so useful to the Comes Britannorium that he would beg the loan of me from my uncle. The faint hope blossomed into determination as I lay there, listening to the creaks and groans of the ship, and the restless slap of the river against her hull.

There is little that travels faster in a seaport town than word of rich patrons and mad quests. I learned of that later for, at first light, my uncle had roused me to accompany him while he bargained for some suitable cargo. Local wine and oil in amphorae, several bales of fine Egyptian cotton cloth and some beautifully tanned and colored Hibernian leather were acquired by mid-morning and my uncle not displeased, though never so much as a word of thanks, much less praise, rewarded my efforts. In truth, I had had no trouble with the corrupt Latin, larded though it was with the wretched Hibernian patois. I was back on board the *Corellia* when the stable lad of the inn came with a message for my uncle from Lord Artos. My uncle scowled as he scanned the scrap of parchment and glanced ominously at me.

"Humph. He's asked for you, boy. Seems I told him of your trick with dialects. He needs your tongue to buy mounts for his journey," my uncle said. "Off you go and use your wits for Lord Artos's sake. Prince Cador would have him assisted in every way, even by such a one as you."

He gave me a light cuff to remind me of my manners and I scrambled off the ship and after the inn lad as fast as I could, before the expression on my face ruined this opportunity. Not only did I know languages, I knew horses. Perhaps my notion of becoming indispensable to Lord Artos had some chance. My uncle had his cargo—with my help. Could I not now become part of this quest for great warrior horses?

The Comes and his Companions had slept late, despite the noise about the busy inn, and had just finished breaking their fast when I rushed in upon them.

"*Ave*, Galwyn, well come," Artos said, expansively gesturing me to their table. It bore little but crumbs and so many empty platters that I suspected his Companions had made up for the three days of meals they'd missed. Lord Artos caught my glance and his grin was mischievous. "Your uncle grudgingly admitted you speak many languages. None of us can make out what it is they speak here. They garble Latin as if they were chewing tough beef. Signs suffice in ordering a meal but I'd rather know the price I must pay for decent mounts and to hire a reliable caravan leader."

"My honor, Lord Artos, my honor," I managed to reply, curbing all manner of wild impulses to puff my experience in such matters. I would prove it with deeds, not words.

Once away from the port, Burtigala spread out, sprawling beyond the boundaries of the town originally set up by the Roman governors of the province. The bustling market area was built on the Roman design, despite the cramped tiny stalls that cluttered the space near the slave pens and along the animal fields. There were many people about, and I noticed the Companions staring at the occasional Nubian, black and splendid in richly colored robes; the slim, swart men whose rolling gait marked them as traders from the Levant; the big Goths swaggering an arrogant path through the crowds of small-statured folk. They, in their turn, marked my Lord Artos and his tall, muscular Companions and slowed their pace so that they did not overrun us.

All around was the jabber and liquid sounds of many languages, fragments of which I could identify as we passed the speakers.

"Is it always like this, Galwyn?" Bericus asked, out of the side of his mouth.

"It is, sir, only sometimes much more so."

"More so?" Flavian asked.

"This is not a market day, sir. Or a feast day."

"The Gods have been good," Flavian muttered under his breath.

As soon as we reached the animal market, Baldus Afritus pushed his way forward to meet us, his sizable paunch clearing his path. He wore his oily smile and smoothed his rather soiled robes over his belly. I murmured a *caveat* to Lord Artos.

"Baldus Afritus at your service, noble lord," Baldus said unctuously in his heavily accented Latin, giving a Legion salute which Lord Artos ignored. Baldus now repeated his introduction in an even more garbled Celtic.

"Mounts," Lord Artos answered in Latin, moving to the rails where he cast his eyes over the rugged ponies displayed. "Seven to ride of at least fourteen hands of height, and four pack animals."

The smile on Baldus's face increased as he saw a fat profit for the day. "I have many fine strong ponies that would carry you from here to Rome with no trouble."

I snickered, for by then I had had enough time to assess the sorry condition of these "fine strong ponies," most of them with no flesh on their bones even this late into a fine summer, their hooves untrimmed, their backs scabby with rain rash and their withers white with old sores from badly fitting saddles. Most were so small that Lord Artos's tall men would have to ride with their knees up under their chins.

"And what do you think of Baldus's offerings?" Lord Artos asked me, his eyes slightly narrowed as he gazed at me. Baldus watched me, too. So, as if we were discussing the weather and not the beasts, I gave the Lord my assessment, speaking in our own dear language of which Baldus knew little. I told him that few would last the trip.

"Two only, Lord, the bay with the star and snip, and the brown horse with the off-white sock."

Lord Artos gave a nod and walked on, despite Baldus's protestations, to the next pen which, in truth, contained animals in little better shape. I could almost feel Baldus's stare piercing my shoulder blades. In that lot, a second sturdy brown looked able to carry the weight of one of the Companions as it dozed, hipshot in the sun.

By the end of the day, after much looking, and then considerable checking of teeth and tendons, backs and wind, Lord Artos struck a bargain for four. Baldus and another horse coper vied with each other, promising that more beautiful, strong animals would be brought up from lush pastures further from Burtigala so that the noble Lords would have the most suitable beasts available. I was sent off to arrange for grain, a separate field to store them in, a trustworthy lad to watch them and a farrier to trim their hooves for the journey.

"You've a keen eye, lad," Lord Artos said, laying a friendly arm across my shoulders as he and the Companions made their way back to the inn, "a light hand and a good seat. You're better riding the horses of the land than those of the sea, aren't you?" I could only nod, overwhelmed with delight at his praise. He clapped me companionably. "Will your uncle indulge me with your services for tomorrow as well? That is, after you've ordered a proper meal from this barbarian landlord."

◆   ◆   ◆

That evening, to my surprise and relief, for I had been having a sorry time of it loading cargo with the crew, Bericus came clattering down to the docks, leading one of the ponies purchased that morning.

"There's a merchant, an honest man by the look of him," Bericus said after a courteous greeting to my uncle. "But Lord Artos can make nothing of his speech. May we have the good offices of young Galwyn? My Lord would deem it a great favor."

It was deftly done but I saw Bericus slip something into my uncle's palm which caused him to smile broadly and summarily gesture me to attend the Companion. I was filthy, my cheek bloodied from a crate that happened to slip, and limping from another that had been purposely dumped on my foot by my uncle's sailors.

"I cannot go to Lord Artos like this," I said, mortified at my state.

"The Comes cannot wait on you!" my uncle said and, before I realized his intent, he pitched me over the side of the ship. "You'll be clean enough when you've dried off," he bellowed down at me.

Bericus said nothing but he wheeled and, back on the dock, reached down to haul me out of the water. I was some cleaner, it was true, and somewhat mollified that Bericus scowled at such treatment of me. The ride on the bright summer's evening, long enough to dry the thin tunic I wore, was also enough to lift my spirits.

Tegidus was the name of the merchant and his language

was Gallic, though of a dialect I had heard but once before, in my father's house many years before. He, too, wished to buy horses at Septimania though his search was not for the same breed as ours. *Ours indeed! How brash I was!* He had trade to exchange as well and he worried about arriving safely in Septimania until he had heard of the Comes Artos and his Companions, so obviously valiant warriors. He had come as far as Burtigala by ship in a fair-sized party, and hoped that, if the Companions joined him, he could start the long journey in two days' time. They had but to finish buying mounts and pack animals, as they had brought their own supplies.

"I believe the man," Lord Artos said, smoothing his beard around his smile. "What is your opinion, young Galwyn?"

"Mine, sir?"

"Do you think him honest?"

"He is who he says he is, Lord Artos, for my father had dealings with the man many years ago. I remember the name, and that the dealings were well conducted."

"Tell Tegidus that we would be glad to join him and his band, and we will set out tomorrow as soon as we have mounts."

"My lord, we could go now to the farm and buy the ponies from the herder before Baldus increases the price, as he will, if he knows there is a demand."

Lord Artos peered at the darkening sky. "Is there time?"

"Enough if you ride now!"

The twinkle returned to the Comes's eyes and his beard framed a wide smile. "Inform Tegidus of your suggestion. We can offer him a mount to accompany us."

Bericus procured torches from the landlord and the four of us were mounted and riding down the road in less time than it takes to tell it. We roused the herder from a bed he was loath to leave; he stood in the doorway, scratching himself.

"I've an early start in the morning to the market at Burtigala," he whined but brightened when he heard Tegidus clink his bag of coin.

"Perhaps we can save you that long journey and provide more profit than you would realize from Baldus," I said, winking.

"Ah, that one! Skin you of your hide and sell your meat for beef, he would!"

Granted it is not generally advisable to buy ponies in the dark, but knowing hands can find curb and splint and check hoof, teeth and condition. These were sturdy mountain stock, with flesh on their bones, hard hooves and good frogs, and young enough to be easily resold on return. They were sure of foot, too, for which I was thankful as Bericus and I raced them up and down the hill to test their wind.

Before the glass could be turned for the new day, we left the farm, each leading four well-grown ponies. My arms were nearly pulled out of their sockets by the time we reached Burtigala, my legs ached with the strain of holding me on the withers of my own mount, and my thighs were chafed from the rough saddle pad.

"Are you not the son of Decitus Varianus, the Factor?" Tegidus asked me as we turned the animals out in the rented paddock.

"He was my father." My throat closed at the reminder of happier days.

"Ah! The little lad who chirped so happily in any language he heard." Tegidus's white-toothed smile was briefly illuminated by the sputtering torches. "I was sorry to hear of your father's death, lad. You are well employed with Lord Artos but you have been more than helpful to an old friend this day." He tucked something in my hand which I, in turn, lodged in my belt, too weary to dispute the unnecessary vail or set his notion of my employment to rights.

I do not recall how but I seem to have spent the night in Lord Artos's chamber, on a pallet by the foot of the bed he shared with Flavian and Bericus.

Knowing that the loading of the *Corellia* continued that morning, I was somewhat concerned for my absence.

"Nonsense, lad," Lord Artos said. "Flavian will return with you to spare you reproaches, but you have been of invaluable assistance to me, which is as Prince Cador charged your uncle. You have done no wrong."

When we reached the ship, the crew were already busy hauling bales and amphorae up the gangplank. But my uncle's expression when he saw me gave me pause, though it turned courteous enough when he bowed and smiled at Flavian.

"You have our thanks, lad," Flavian said loudly as I handed over the rein of the pony I had ridden. As he took the lead from me, he pressed some coins in my hand, grinned and winked, then clattered off, his long legs dangling almost to his mount's knees.

Hastily, I concealed the coins in my belt, to keep Tegidus's offering company. Just in time, too, for my uncle was hauling me by the ear back up the plank, cursing under his breath.

"Your fine friends are gone now, lad, and you'll do the work you are hired for."

I do not know what put my uncle in such a bad mood for I *had* done the work I was hired for in dealing for the cargo. Still I had to help load. It was a weary, weary day with cuffs and blows and kicks to speed me at my tasks. I did my best but sometimes it seemed they left the most unwieldy lots for me, heavy beyond my strength, and then laughed as I strained and heaved with little avail. I paid dearly that day for those hours with Lord Artos. I would have paid twice the price had it been asked.

I was so exhausted by nightfall that I could not summon the energy to eat. Instead I crept into a space between deck and cargo where few could find me. In the dark, I transferred the coins and the gold ring Tegidus has given me into my worn empty pouch and tucked all safely back under my belt. As soon as I laid my head down, I was asleep.

The cold roused me, even buffered as I was between bundles and deck. The clammy sort of cold that suggests a dense fog. Groaning, I realized that my uncle's humor—for he had planned to sail with the morning tide—would scarcely improve. I could not stay hidden all day, however preferable. When I heard the others stirring and grumbling at the weather, I crept out, shivering. Hunger drove me to the galley and, though I did snatch a few pieces of bread, the cook had other tasks for me. I was sent for supplies from the after-hold. I was struggling with a sack of the beans he intended to soak for the evening meal when the little pouch fell from my belt.

The first mate saw it, and snatched it up. "Ah, what have we here? Light-fingered is he, too, this bastard scum of a Celt?"

I do not know what prompted me, save that I had had enough of him, and of my miserable existence on the *Corellia* with only the prospect of more of the same until my spirit was completely broken.

Because he held the pouch aloft, dangling from the draw-strings, I saw my chance. I leaped, catching the pouch, and in another leap, dove over the side of the ship, swimming through the still water and losing myself in the mist. Even the shouts and curses from shipboard were quickly muffled in that thick fog. When my first frantic strokes exhausted me, I tread the water, terrified that perhaps I had swum in the wrong direction. Some early-morning garbage bobbed about me and, listening avidly, I heard the unmistakable lap of water against a shore, and struck out toward the sound.

I hauled myself out, gasping for breath and shivering in the raw air but filled with a sort of triumph. I had escaped! I would join Lord Artos. He would have me. Had he not said that I was useful to him with my gift of tongues? He would need someone to interpret Tegidus on the long road they would travel together. He would surely need my skills at Septimania.

I opened the purse to count my worldly wealth and found

it far more than I had expected. Several small coins of the sort we use in Briton and two, not one, gold rings that traders carry, current in any port. I could scarcely believe such good fortune and generosity. This should prove enough—and I knew how to haggle—to buy a warm cloak and leggings as well as a pony from the farmer. I knew the one I wanted, too small for most men to ride, but the right size for me.

None of the traders in the market place, glad of any dealings on such a foggy morning, questioned my wealth or my reasons. I managed to buy some travel bread and grain.

By the time I reached the farm, the fog still held the coastline in its white roll. But the little pony I had noted grazed in the meadow. The farmer was in an expansive mood, having sold his best at a good profit to Tegidus and Lord Artos with no need for recourse to a villain like Baldus. He was quite willing to sell me the pony for, as I was quick to point out, it was indeed too short in the leg to suit a man of any tribe. Out of kindness, he patched together a bridle of sorts and showed me how to wrap the folds of my cloak to make a pad.

I trotted off up the road, certain that Lord Artos would not be far ahead of me. By evening, when I had met few travelers and none I liked the look of, I was having doubts about the whole venture. I ate my travel bread by a stream well off the track, and curled up in my cloak, the pony hobbled in a fair patch of grass. I spent an uneasy night. The ground had this tendency to roll beneath me and I kept waking in a fright that I was still aboard the *Corellia*.

•   •   •

It took me three days to catch up with Lord Artos. They were making camp and someone had successfully hunted for a kettle which burbled with appetizing odors on its tripod over a good hot fire.

Tegidus saw me first, rushing up to me, gesticulating wildly, his expression both welcoming and anxious. "The oak has answered my prayers, for I should not have undertaken this journey so cheerfully if I had known you would not be among their number."

"Lord Artos, it is Galwyn come to rescue us from ignorance!" Bericus roared. Before I knew it, my pony and I were ringed by the other Companions who pulled me one way or the other.

"Your uncle relented then?" Lord Artos said as he waded through the importunate crowd. He did not stop to hear what my answer might have been and so I never had to give him a lie at all. "By God's eye, I'm glad enough to see you. Signs, signals and smiles do not make good communications. You are well come, young Galwyn, well come indeed."

"Artos says that our animals are overloaded," Tegidus's men complained to me. "He will not let us cook a midday meal and insists that we all take our turn at watch at night. That is why we travel with him. So that he may guard."

"Those fools have packed their animals so badly that half have sores," was Bericus's plaint, "and they will not attend when we show them how to rearrange the loads properly."

It took only a few minutes to explain, each to the other, what was amiss, and set it right. Then, to my everlasting joy, Lord Artos encircled my shoulder with his great arm and led me to their campfire. No matter if I was listed as a runaway apprentice by my spiteful uncle, I would gladly spend the rest of my life on a galley bench to have the mark of Lord Artos's favor now. Flavian himself heaped me a huge plate of the rabbit stew which did much to quiet my stomach. And I did not have to stand watch or help the cooks—at least that first night.

The journey to Septimania was not without its trials, unusual icy storms being the least of them and steep and rough roads the worst, but all of us, bar one packmule, arrived safely at our destination and had two days to rest before the Great Sale officially started.

It was truly a wonder of the world to see so many fine horses, of all breeds and colors and uses, picketed about the great field. To watch the beautiful horses perform their paces and leap rough barriers as easily as a deer and listen—for me to report to Lord Artos—to what was said.

We camped slightly apart but near enough to Tegidus's site to continue the protection agreed upon. I picked up the camp jargon quickly enough and so learned which horse dealers could be trusted not to disguise the faults of their wares. But what Lord Artos needed was visible enough—strong, wide-hipped mares with strong foals at foot, with good bone and a fine sheen to dark hide beneath their fuzzy birth coats. Great, deep-barreled stallions, powerful and aggressive, full of spirit and seed, trumpeting their virility all through the night and attempting to mount any mare in season wherever she was in the camp. I don't think I slept more than an hour at a time, nor missed the lack during the excitement of the days until Lord Artos had the sixteen mares and four stallions.

He sold off the unneeded ponies, mounting his men, and me, on his new purchases. He kept my little pony, as much he said, because he could not peremptorily sell off my uncle's property. I contrived not to look in his direction at that. The pony was truly mine, bought with gratuities, but now was not the time to mention that fact. But there was a further reason: Even the most unbiddable of the stallions—so wild he had had to be roped, tied and twitched before a round bit could be inserted between his snapping jaws and a stout bridle attached to his head—was unexpectedly calmed in my pony's company. The sight of that little imp, who could easily stand beneath the stallion—and did during the worst of the rains—was as ludicrous as it was beneficial.

The big mare which I now bestrode was nowhere near as comfortable as my short-coupled pony and she had a foal at foot besides, a well-grown colt of some three or four months by then, who was ready up to nip my legs or heels if he felt I was interfering with his feeding. His dam was so broad in the withers I could barely get my legs around her and felt split apart when she trotted. Whereas the mate and his crew would have laughed their sides sore to see me, the Companions' smiles were good-natured and not at my expense.

The stallions took handling and I was glad that I was relegated to the more placid-tempered mares. The stallions needed the firm hand and strong legs of the Companions to

115

keep them in order. Flavius and Bericus were considerable horsemen, the other Companions no less so. But Lord Artos was their superior, sitting lightly balanced on the mad black demon's back, swaying slightly from the hips as the stallion cavorted or reared or bucked, objecting to the slightest unusual object on the track.

Sometimes I think we travelled farther sideways and backwards than forwards and yet, we made good time on the return trip and reached Burtigala on a fine bright warm afternoon. From my vantage point on my big mare (either my legbones had grown or they had been permanently stretched a handspan longer, but she was easier to bestride), I anxiously scanned the ships anchored offshore or tied up at the dock for any sight of the *Corellia*, but to my intense relief she was not in port.

I had lost track of the actual days and each morning roused with that cold weight of fear that she had made port in the night and I would have a reckoning with my uncle to face. During the day I was too busy to think. Prince Cador had requisitioned two fat ships in which the Comes could ship his all-important mares and stallions across the Narrow Sea.

We had some time, I can tell you, getting the horses into their berths. I thought we'd lose the biggest stallion, even with my little fellow to bear him company in the same stall. He nearly got a nail through his skull, rearing against the planks as they were pounded down about the four horses in that first boat. He had me dangling from the end of his lead chain like a rat in a bullterrier's jaws. Then Lord Artos thought to blindfold him and, unable to see, he was more tractable. At least until we were in the following swells of the Narrow Sea.

We discovered, in the worst way possible, that horses can get seasick. The stallion covered me with it, though my little pony, his eyes white with fear, all four legs poked out stiffly, did not succumb. Yet it was not a rough crossing and both ships stayed within sight of each other the entire way. Bericus and Flavian, who sailed with me, were rather heartened by their performance but, truth to tell, we were all so busy with the horses, soothing them, cleaning up after them, coaxing them to eat the fragrant hay, that we humans had no time to be sick.

Lord Artos inspected the horses morning, noon and night, and had himself rowed across to the second ship to perform the same office as soon as he was done with ours. Never was I more relieved to see Isca Dumnorium on the horizon than that afternoon.

"You'll be on land before dark, my lad," I murmured to the stallion, standing with his head bowed between his splayed front legs, his finely shaped ears drooping to either side of his elegant head, his black coat grimed and rough with sweat though we had groomed him morning and night. Remembering his fine displays on land, it was disheartening to see his proud spirit so low. Then his head lifted suddenly and his nostrils flared as he smelled land.

I could have wished his spirits had taken slightly longer to revive, for he proved his old self when the deck planks were removed and he could see daylight and knew himself near land. He trumpeted like a wild thing, pawing and thrashing at his tethers. I used my own tunic to cover his eyes but they hoisted the pony ashore first, then the stallion, and the two mares.

The stallion was weak, though, from the journey and had trouble keeping his legs under him. He had an apprehensive look on his face as he staggered first this way and then that, recovering landlegs.

"*Ave,* Comes Artos," cried a glad voice and Prince Cador himself came riding down to the dock. "Magnificent, Comes Britannorium!" he exclaimed as he dismounted, throwing his reins to an aide. Appraisingly, he circled the stallion, his face expressing his high opinion. "Truly magnificent. Sixteen hands high if he's one!"

"Sixteen hands and a bit more," Lord Artos said. "Look at the bone of him, the breadth of his barrel, the power in his haunches. Oh, he's gaunt enough from three days at sea but we'll put condition on him soon enough once he's at Deva."

"By the Gods, the mares're up to him as well!" Prince Cador's bright light eyes widened as the first mare was set on her feet on the shore. Bericus was at her side, giving her sufficient mass to lean against while she scattered her front legs. Then she whinnied wildly for her foal who was already thrashing about in the hoist sling, nickering frantically for reassurance.

The Prince clouted Lord Artos affectionately on the shoulder. "I believe you now, Artos, for I had my doubts before, I'll be frank. But these are splendid animals." Then he leaned

He had me dangling from the end of his lead chain
like a rat in a bullterrier's jaws.

closer to the Comes. "How long do you think it will be before we all can be mounted on such war horses as these?"

I was struck by the look that suffused the features of the Comes Britanniorum, that look of far-seeing: not of trance or dream but of a reality waiting just ahead of him.

"Five, six, seven years and there won't be a warrior without a black horse of this quality to carry him to battle against the Saxons."

"Aye, the Saxons!" And the Prince's expression turned grim. He pulled Artos to one side for private conversation and, out of the corner of my eye—for I was busy feeding the mare hanks of grass pulled from the roadside, I could see all the elation of success bleed from the Comes's face. I was saddened to see the change.

Suddenly my shoulder was seized in a fierce and painful grip and, startled, I tried first to twist free, and then to see who had made me captive.

"I have you, Galwyn Varianus!" Dolcenus bellowed and there was no escaping the grip of the big and burly Port Officer. "Scurrilous wretch! Runaway apprentice! You'll come with me, vile ingrate, and stay in the lockup until your uncle returns."

It was too late for me to rue my own stupidity. I should have known that Dolcenus would arrive to see what manner of strange cargo was being hoisted ashore in his precinct. I would have been safe aboard the ship. Now my brave adventure was at an end and I could almost feel the manacles of a galley slave tightening about my wrists.

It was in fact Bericus's huge hand, rough with sword and

rein callous that prevented Dolcenus from hauling me summarily away. That and the now frightened mare whose lead rope I still held. She reared and Dolcenus released me, shouting at the top of his lungs for me to be recaptured immediately, shouting for help in this resistance to his authority.

"What goes?" I heard Lord Artos cry.

"If you harm one of those mares, Dolcenus . . ." Prince Cador shouted.

And the mare reared again. Fortunately, Bericus was beside me and together we calmed her, despite the shouts and imprecations that colored the air. Her alarm had infected the stallion and the pony who were nickering and reacting to the general confusion. I had to dance out of the way of the colt foal who was trying to get under his dam's belly for safety.

It took the combined authority of both Prince and Comes Artos to restore order, hear Dolcenus's charge against me while I stood, head down, too humiliated to look beyond the belts of the men encircling me.

"It was my understanding," Lord Artos said when Dolcenus paused in his litany of my sins to draw breath, "that Captain Gralior dispatched the boy to be of assistance in our journey. In truth, he had already been of great help. Knowing that Gralior was due to sail, I had asked if I might have the loan of the boy—for his knowledge of so many barbarous languages—while Gralior was at sea. How was it, Galwyn, that you joined us?"

When I could not answer, Comes Artos put his hand under my chin and forced me to look at him. Unmanly tears trickled down my cheeks and I could not speak for fear of blubbering.

"He came on a pony, with a travel cloak and leggings," Bericus said stoutly. I felt his encouraging hand on my shoulderblade, one hard thumb poking me to speak.

"He's a thief as well?" cried Dolcenus. "Branded he must be!"

"Nonsense," Prince Cador said. "I knew the boy's father. Too honorable a family to breed thieves. Speak up, lad."

"Aye, speak, lad," and Lord Artos's voice was as kind as his eyes when I dared glance at them.

"I bought the pony with the small gold ring Tegidus thanked me with."

"You see, Dolcenus, this boy's no thief!" said Bericus.

"And the cloak and leggings with the coins you were kind enough to send me, Lord Artos. Please, I want to serve *you,* Comes Britannorium," and I dropped to my knees in the dust, as much because my legs would no longer hold me up as to humbly plead my cause. "It is the horses of the land that I know, not the sea!"

"Is the boy a free man?" Lord Artos asked Dolcenus.

The man sputtered and stammered.

"Yes, my lord, I am free. I was only apprenticed to my uncle, not enslaved." I glared at Dolcenus to make him speak the truth.

"That is correct," Prince Cador said when Dolcenus still would not speak in his frustration. "I remember the case of Decitus Varianus now. He acted honorably in his circumstances."

"The boy's too good with his tongue to lose him to a barge captain, Lord Artos," said Bericus. "And he's got a fine way with seasick horses!"

"Horses!" cried Lord Artos, grabbing me up from the ground. "We can just make the evening tide if we hurry. Bericus, you stay here and see these safely on the way to Deva. Cador, make what provision is needed to salve the uncle's wounded pride. Young Galwyn, you come with me!"

We made a swift passage back to Burtigala with both ships but that return voyage was rougher and took its toll on men and beasts. I was far too busy looking after the mares and my Lord Artos to have time to be seasick. The final return voyage was the best and the worst: the best because Lord Artos put me in charge of the horses on one ship (Flavian was on the other) and I was both proud of the honor and fearful of failure: the worst because we caught the brunt of a fierce autumnal gale for the first two days. Somehow we, and the horses, survived, though all of us were badly battered. With tattered sails, the two ships limped into Isca Dumnorium.

Lord Artos's face broke into a great smile when I shouted to him that all the horses were alive.

"Galwyn," he said, when we had the beasts safely on the shore, "had I more men like you, we'd drive the Saxons forever from our lands."

"I thought, Lord Artos, it was the horses you needed to do that," I said, so relieved that I hazarded an impudence.

"The horses need men to ride them, Galwyn: men such as

you!" And he clamped his great hand on my shoulder, his eyes gleaming with his fervor.

"Then," I replied, dropping to my knee and bringing the hem of his garment to my forehead in an act of fealty, "I am your man Comes Britannorium!"

And I was, serving Lord Artos all the days of his life and riding the black horses of the King until the end of mine.

So light was his lordly heart, and a little
    boyish;
His life he liked lively—the less he cared
To be lying for long, or long to sit,
So busy his young blood, his brain so wild,
And also a point of pride pricked him in
    heart,
For he nobly had willed, he would never eat
On so high a holiday, till he heard first
Of some fair feat or fray some far-borne
    tale,
Of some marvel of might . . .

from *Sir Gawain and the Green Knight,*
translated by Marie Borroff

Holly and Ivy

James D. Macdonald
and Debra Doyle

It was New Year's Day at Camelot, and banners snapped on the breeze above the many towers. The castle's drawbridge was down, for under the rule of King Arthur Pendragon all Britain was at peace.

Sir Gawain of Orkney walked briskly across the castle courtyard toward the Great Hall. After a New Year's morning spent in chapel, and an afternoon of dancing, Gawain was more than ready for the evening feast. In fact he was hungry enough to eat a dragon, scales and all, and not ask for sauce.

As Gawain approached the feast-hall, the high double doors swung open a foot or so as another of Arthur's knights came out into the chilly courtyard. The newcomer was Sir Kay the Seneschal, Arthur's foster-brother and the manager of the king's household.

The seneschal's expression was fixed in a respectful smile

under his bristling orange mustaches. As soon as the hall doors swung shut, the smile slipped.

"Son of a wizard-glamored troll!" Kay yelled, and slammed his fist into the stone wall. "The hairy little wart isn't ever going to forget that I used to beat him up regularly when I thought he was just my baby brother!"

"Ah, some problem?" Gawain asked. Kay looked up from where he was banging his head against the wall.

"Since the seige and assault was ceased at Troy," Kay began in strangled tones, "no knight has eaten before the king has started his meal. It's courtesy."

"I know that, Kay," said Gawain patiently. Inside the feast-hall, by now, the servers would be pacing up and down between the holly-decked tables, passing out trenchers, pouring wine and beer, and filling the silver bowls with apples and nuts. His stomach growled in anticipation. "So what's the problem?"

"It's Arthur," Kay went on. "He's not going to eat until he's seen a marvel." The seneschal paused, and cast a glance up to heaven. "If a feast ever started on time around here, now *that* would be a flaming marvel!"

"Come, now," Gawain said. "It can't be as bad as all that."

"Oh, yes it can," said Kay. He pushed himself away from the wall and started across the courtyard. "I've got to go to the kitchen and tell the cook to hold dinner until my five-times-forsaken foster brother gets his blasted miracle!"

"Maybe there's some way to fix this," said Gawain. "I'll come with you." He grabbed a passing footpage. "Go to Sir

Holly and Ivy

Dynadan, give him my compliments and all that, and ask him to please meet me in the kitchen at once." The boy hurried away, and Gawain strode off toward the kitchen in the seneschal's wake.

"I tell you, this is one feast that's going to turn out right," the head cook began as Kay stomped into the warm, fragrant kitchen with Gawain at his heels. "The pork is done to a turn, the split-pea soup for the second course is almost ready, and the hot fritters are going into the fat right now."

"Well, tell the servers they'll have to wait," said Kay. "Slow everything you can slow, and stop frying those fritters."

"But they'll get soggy!"

"Then dip 'em in honey and call 'em dessert!" snarled Kay. "The king won't start the feast until he's seen a marvel. Unless you have a marvel on tap that I don't know about, we may all starve to death."

"I can walk on my hands and whistle at the same time," the cook offered hopefully.

"No, not marvelous enough," said Kay with a sour expression. "Now get back to work—if the pork gets burnt, we all know whose fault it's going to be, and it won't be His Glorious Majesty's, I can tell you that!"

The head cook dashed away, kitchen boys scattering around him, even as the side door opened and Sir Dynadan came in.

"Dynadan," said Gawain, "you're the Jester Knight, and the quickest wit in Camelot. We need an idea in a hurry if we're going to eat."

127

Dynadan looked about the kitchen. "I see food all over the place," he said. "What's holding it up?"

"My uncle the king wants to see a marvel," said Gawain, before Kay could answer. The seneschal's always ruddy features had been growing redder by the minute. By now they had taken on a color like that of the beet tarts that rested on a table near the great hearth.

Dynadan shook his head. "A marvel . . . I haven't seen one of those in years."

"Nor I," said Gawain. "Now, if the Carle of Carlisle or the Loathly Lady were here, that would be a horse of a different color—but they don't make wonders like that anymore."

"Maybe I should just cut my own head off," said Kay gloomily. "Maybe *then* he'd be happy."

"Horse of a different color . . . head cut off . . ." murmured Dynadan. "By Saint Loy, I think we have something! Who has a white horse we could paint?"

"White?" asked Kay. "Lancelot du Lak. Mucking great charger—the Marshal's always coming to me about running out of oats for the beast."

"But would Lance let us play with his steed?" Gawain asked.

"That besotted Frenchman would ride in a cart if he thought it would get him to dinner," said Kay. The seneschal grabbed a scullery-maid by one arm. "You—find Sir Lancelot and get him in here." He turned back to Dynadan. "All right, you'll get your horse."

"Good," said Dynadan. "Tell Cook to take the pea soup off the fire. We're going to need it."

A moment later, Sir Lancelot walked in. "How may I help you? And what has happened to the feast, you know?" Despite years at Arthur's court, his French accent was still thicker than the split-pea soup. "There are twelve dishes before each pair, and still the king does not, how do you say it, give them the cue to start."

"He's waiting for a marvel," said Gawain.

Lancelot's brow wrinkled. "A marvel? These English . . ."

"A marvel," said Dynadan. "And you, my friend, are going to be part of it." He handed the tall Frenchman the pot of split-pea soup. "Here—take this glop and smear it all over your horse."

"I? Paint my horse? *Sacre bleu!*"

Gawain shook his head. "No, Lance, *vert*. Green. Now get going."

Sir Lancelot took the cooling pot of thick green soup, and left with it.

"Now we need a basket or something I can fix up to look like a head," said Dynadan.

"What's that for?" Gawain asked.

"Part of the joke," explained Dynadan. "What could be more marvelous than a giant on a green horse riding into court, having Gawain cut his head off, and riding out again?"

Kay pointed to a butter-tub standing in one corner of the kitchen. "There. Use that."

"Beautiful," said Dynadan. "It'll do fine." Within minutes, he had painted the wooden tub with more of the pea soup. He drew a crude face on one side with charcoal, and daubed on beet custard for the mouth and the bright red cheeks. Inspired by Dynadan's efforts, Gawain went out into the courtyard and returned with holly and ivy he'd pulled down from the Yuletide garlands. The green leaves and vines made a fine crop of beard and hair for the grinning butter-tub.

Kay shook his head. "Arthur's never going to believe this is real."

"He doesn't have to think it's real," said Dynadan. "Just marvelous. After all, he's probably getting hungry too."

"You don't know him like I do," muttered Kay. "He'd fast from now until Easter, just to make a point."

Sir Lancelot came back into the kitchen as Dynadan and Gawain were putting the finishing touches on the head.

"My horse, he is now green," said the Frenchman, "and so are my hands. What more do you wish me to do?"

Gawain pointed at the decorated tub. "Lance, do you think you can ride with this thing fastened on top of your head?"

The French knight looked puzzled. "If you are sure it is for the honor of Camelot, but of course. Why?"

"I'm going to throw my voice," explained Dynadan. "A trick I picked up in the Joyous Gard, along with how to give a hotfoot, short-sheet beds, and balance buckets of water above doorways."

"I'm glad I wasn't along on that adventure," said Gawain. He stood up from where he'd been kneeling with Dynadan while they fixed the butter-tub. "I'll go into the hall, and wait for you and Lance to make your move."

He smiled at Kay. "Don't worry," he told the seneschal. "Arthur will be feasting before you know it."

The sun had gone down and the great hall was lit by torches alone when Gawain and Kay entered. The Orkney knight made his way to the High Table, and took his seat between Queen Guenevere and Sir Agravain de la Dure Main.

"Did I miss anything?" Gawain whispered to his brother out of the side of his mouth.

"It's been as dull as watching soup cool," said Sir Agravain. "Which, coincidentally . . ."

Agravain never finished his sentence. A boom like thunder rolled through the hall.

A great steed came hurtling through the double doors, bearing a huge man on its back. In the flickering torchlight, the effect of Dynadan's trick was far better than Gawain had expected: the horse, dyed green as it was with pea soup, was hardly recognizable as Lancelot's; and the French knight himself, covered with a long green cloak drawn above his head, with the decorated butter-tub adding to his height, seemed almost a giant.

The green face on the tub was incredibly lifelike. The eyes seemed alive, although Gawain knew that he himself had painted them with soot from the bottom of a pot. The heavy hair and beard of holly and ivy covered the joint between Lancelot and the false head so well that Gawain wanted to applaud the effect.

"If this doesn't get the feast started, nothing will," he whispered happily.

Lancelot was holding a great green axe in one green hand. He rode up directly in front of the High Table, and reined his charger to a halt.

"Who's in charge of this mob?" he roared.

Gawain elbowed Sir Agravain. "That Dynadan," he said. "I never thought he could do it. He makes it sound like the head is really talking."

"What?" Agravain said. Gawain's younger brother seemed unable to take his eyes from the strange apparition.

Reminding himself that Agravain wasn't in on the joke, Gawain said shortly, "Nothing." Then he turned back to the show in front of him as Lancelot leapt from his horse and swaggered up and down the aisle between the tables.

"Can this be Arthur's house?" the Green Knight shouted. "Where is your courage?"

On the other side of Queen Guenevere, wood scraped on stone as King Arthur pushed back his chair and stood.

"Fellow," he called, "I am Arthur, King of the Britons, and these are my people. I order you to stay and tell your tale."

"I don't have the time to waste on beardless boys," bellowed the voice of the green man. "I had hoped to find warriors here to play a game with me, but I doubt any have the heart to trade a blow for a blow. Your champion may strike me first, and then I'll hit him second!"

For a long moment, silence fell over the hall. Even the musicians stopped playing. Kay bent forward, over Gawain's shoulder. "That's your cue," he said.

Gawain sprang to his feet. "*I* will face you!" he exclaimed, vaulting over the table to stand in front of the Green Knight. He winked broadly in the direction of the figure's throat, where Lancelot would be watching.

"Excellent," came the voice. "Then take my axe, and cut off my head."

"Are you quite sure?" Gawain called, making certain that everyone in the hall could hear. No sense having the people in the back miss the byplay. "With your head off, you won't be able to strike at me."

In reply, Lancelot handed the axe to Gawain, and knelt. Gawain took the axe in both hands, raised it high, and swept it down—being careful to hit the tub and not the man hidden inside the cloak. Just as it should, the tub came off and rolled across the floor.

Lancelot groped for the head, grasped it by the twining ivy hair, and pushed himself back to his feet. Dynadan's voice rang out again, seeming to come from the head that Lancelot was holding at arm's length by the holly hair.

"Well then, Sir Gawain, meet me a year from today at the Green Chapel, that I may give you back your blow!"

Gawain almost choked with holding in his laughter. He returned to his seat at High Table as Lancelot, the butter-tub still in one hand, vaulted into the saddle and galloped from the hall, his horse's shoes striking sparks from the flagstones.

Gawain looked over at the King. Arthur's face was a mask of wonder mixed with shock.

"Let the feast begin!" the king finally said, when he got his voice back.

"That was great. We didn't lose much time," Kay whispered to Gawain. "I'm going to go back to the kitchen and tell them to start serving."

"I'll come with you," said Gawain, wiping tears of laughter from his eyes. "Lance will be getting out of costume there, and I want to congratulate him and Dynadan on a job well done."

Down in the kitchen, Dynadan and Lancelot were waiting. Lancelot wore his tub balanced on his head again. Gawain noticed that in the well-lit kitchen it didn't look as realistic as it had in the torchlight above. In fact, Lancelot's features looked ridiculous peeking out from below the collar of his cloak.

"We're ready any time you are," Sir Dynadan said. "I'm hungry."

"When do you want me to enter?" Lancelot asked.

"That . . . that wasn't you in the hall?" Gawain asked, his smile fading from his face.

"But of course not," said Lancelot with a puzzled frown. "What do you mean?"

"We've been waiting in here for you to send word that all was ready," said Dynadan.

Gawain looked closely at Dynadan, to see if he had the twinkle in his eye that meant he was engaged in another jest. Nothing. For once Dynadan was serious. And it was well known that Lancelot was incapable of telling a lie. Whatever had ridden into the feast hall, it hadn't been this homemade giant.

With horrifying clarity Gawain remembered the words

Lancelot, the buttertub still in one hand, vaulted into the saddle and
galloped from the hall.

that the severed head had spoken, as it dangled from the Green Knight's massive fist: "Meet me a year from today at the Green Chapel, that I may give you back your blow!"

Gawain sank back into a chair. "Don't worry about it," he said to Sir Dynadan. "Arthur has already started the feast, so we don't need to play our joke."

"Come, then," said Lancelot, stripping off the cloak and the fake head and flinging them into a corner of the kitchen. "I need to find a seat at table quickly, before the food is gone."

"Take my place," Gawain whispered. "I've lost my appetite."

. . . the Archbishop of Canterbury came forward to protest: "Sir Mordred, do not you fear God's displeasure? First you have falsely made yourself king; now you . . . try to marry your father's wife! If you do not revoke your evil deeds I shall curse you with bell, book, and candle."

"Fie on you! Do your worst!" Sir Mordred replied.

"Sir Mordred, I warn you take heed! or the wrath of the Lord will descend upon you."

from *Le Morte d'Arthur* by
Sir Thomas Malory

The Raven

Nancy Springer

I am Mordred, speaking to you with a bird's thin black tongue. I am Mordred, and it is no easier to say now than it ever was. Even hundreds of years ago, when I was a human and young, when I first came wide-eyed to Camelot, it was hard to be who I was: Mordred, the shadow everyone wanted to forget, the bad seed, King Arthur's doom.

He had made a serious mistake, you see, in begetting me upon my mother, Queen Morgause. All men make mistakes, some worse than others, but Arthur was not just a man. He was the king. It was a strange, exalted and terrible thing, to be King Arthur. When he made mistakes, the sky clouded, the corn grew short, women wept, hundreds of men marched into battle. Whatever he did sent out echoes like a great bell. And because he had sinned, there was a fate on him, and I was its dark right hand.

I knew all this when I first went to court with my brothers as an unblooded knight, a youth of sixteen summers, when I first saw his face.

There he sat at his place upon the rim of the Round Table, King Arthur, and by that time he had ruled for two decades. My half-brother Gawain had been serving him for nearly as many years as I was old. Yet when Gawain presented me, King Arthur turned to me the face of a young man at the height of his powers. There was no gray dulling the bronze of his beard, and the hair of his head curled as golden as his crown. He held his chin high. His gray eyes blazed into me like those of a falcon, regal. He was all that a king should be, and what was more to me, he was a man any day-dreaming boy would choose as a father.

Now that those times are long gone I can admit that I wanted to call him father—and not so much for the sake of his throne as for his own goodliness. I wanted to lay claim to everything that was noble about him, because all the world knew there was very little that was noble in me.

"Mordred," he said as I knelt before him, "welcome."

I was his son, and we both knew it, but he did not acknowledge me. All his life until I caused its end he did not acknowledge me. He could not. He was the king, and had he called me his son the land of his kingdom might have blackened, the water of its lakes might have boiled and turned to poison. So he did not say, "Son." But neither did he scant me his courtesy.

"Ask of me a boon," he told me, "and I will grant it to you."

I blinked, and my mouth came open foolishly, for this was

more than customary courtesy. "But—but Sire," I stammered, "I have earned no reward."

"You are Gawain's brother. Is that not worthiness enough? Speak."

Still on my knees, I stared mutely back at him. Years before, that old son of the devil Merlin had told him plainly that his kingdom was to fall to me and he was to die at my hands in battle. Yet here I was at his court, within arm's reach of him, and he welcomed me with a gift because I was Gawain's brother.

Gawain did not kneel, but stood by my side, and when I glanced up at him he was smiling a little, proudly. His face, weathered and rugged and ruddy, seemed very different than mine, which was smooth and closed and dark. It was hard for anyone to believe he was my brother, even a half-brother.

"My king," he said, "there is no need for such words."

"There is every need. It is seldom enough I give you the soft words you deserve." The king turned to me, motioning me to my feet. "Of all my knights, Mordred, your brother Gawain is the one I most greatly trust. If I had to take my soul out of my body and give it to someone for safekeeping, he would be that man."

"My liege," Gawain protested.

"It is true."

"But you need not say it."

"I am the king, and I will say what I like."

It was simplest fact, yet he was joking. He and Gawain were grinning at each other. These jokes and understandings between people, they were a thing I did not comprehend, they made me feel cold and lacking inside.

Glancing at me, the king remarked to Gawain, "Does your brother never smile?"

"No, liege," Gawain replied. "In truth, he does not."

"But that cannot be. Mordred?" The king turned to me, quizzical. "A little smile?"

I tried, but knew I only bared my teeth like a dog instead. It would have been better not to try. Hiding the effort with a bow, I found my voice and begged, "Sire, may I ask the boon of you some other time?"

"Do so."

It was then, leaving his presence, that I felt for the first time how much I hated what I was fated to be: Mordred the murderer. And the murdered. By the accident of my birth I was as doomed as my king, doomed to lose my life and my soul.

"I should not be here," I said to Gawain. "I should go home."

"Nonsense, boy." He was far older than I, and though he wished me well there was no close understanding between us. Like Gaheris and Gareth, my older brothers, and like my guardian, King Lot, he acted as if the prophecies were of no account, turning to me a smiling face as if he hoped for the best from me.

And now King Arthur was doing much the same—but clear-eyed, knowing quite well what he risked. He was all made of generous courage, and I wished his courage were in me. It should have been. I was his son.

"I mean it," I said to Gawain. "I should leave. No good can come of my being here."

"Do you want to hide yourself away all your life? No brother of mine is a coward."

"I would like to do what is right."

"You just hold up your head and let 'right' take care of itself."

In the courtyard, as Gawain and I came out of the king's tower, a blind harper was sitting and playing on his harp. On his shoulder was perched a raven, a wise bird with a great black heavy bill that made me think of an executioner's ax. The harper did not see me, of course, and played on, chanting a lay about a hero gloriously slain. But the raven saw me and croaked, "Branded, branded! Red handed!" Those who had gathered to hear the harper laughed at its cheekiness, but I shivered, for I felt as if it spoke straight to me.

Putting the bold face to it, I stood with the others and listened to the harper's chanting. Or half listened, for I was thinking. King Arthur had given me a boon after all, not knowing it. He had gifted me with words, and with thoughts.

If I had to take my soul out of my body and give it to someone for safekeeping . . .

If I had to take my soul out of my body . . .

Could this truly be done? It might mean an answer to my pain.

No, I told myself, *no.* It would be the coward's way out. There had to be something of King Arthur's nobility in me. I would stay at his court, and I would strive to become more like him. I would fight my fate.

◆　◆　◆

Days passed. The blind harper left Camelot and moved on to some other castle somewhere in Cornwall. Weeks passed, and months. I acquitted myself as a knight, sometimes well, sometimes badly. I drew blood, and bled some too. Sir Lancelot saved my life once, and I am sure often regretted it afterward. I managed to save no one except myself—sometimes. I took my seat at the Round Table, jousted in tourneys, met Queen Guinevere and many other lovely women. The queen I did not much like, for she reminded me of my mother, who had become a witch. In fact, my mother had learned witchcraft while I was in her womb, which may be why I never learned to smile, and why none of the ladies smiled on me.

As for King Arthur, I saw him as often as anyone did, and ate at his side sometimes, and found no fault with him in his dealings with anyone. He was a bold, great-hearted king, a liege worth dying for.

I knew I did not wish to die for him. But neither did I wish to destroy him.

How I ached to my soul through those long days and weeks and months. I tried to be brave. I told myself a prophecy was a thing of no substance, a specter made only of words, an echo in the wind. But in my heart I knew that words were of all things most powerful. I could feel the words pulsing dark in my blood as I tried to sleep; I could feel them lying heavy in my stomach as I tried to eat; I could feel them waiting in my bones, part of me. My soul struggled against them, but my soul could not pull the black marrow out of my bones.

The Raven

A year passed. I grew soul-weary of fighting fate, and the blind harper came back to Camelot.

Such people often see more clearly than those with eyes. So as he sat one morning in the sun of the courtyard, alone except for the raven on his shoulder, I went and sat next to him.

"Pretty boy," the raven greeted me. I ignored it.

"Do you know who I am?" I challenged the harper.

He replied without hesitation, "You are one who does not smile."

"Do you know why?"

"Because you know how the song must end." His milky eyes stared straight ahead, and his hands strummed softly at his harp. As if he did not care what I might do if he angered me, he said, "You are a fool to be troubled. Do you not know that all songs must end? Waves crest, then break themselves on the sand. Kings reign in glory, then die. There is no beauty in anything without ending."

This was scant comfort. I sat silent.

"There is this, also," the harper added in a voice like the stirring of dry grass, "that the best songs end as they began. And there is this, that when you were very young, a babe in arms, King Arthur tried to kill you. He ordered you set adrift in an open boat on the cold sea. But the boat washed ashore, and you were saved."

I shrugged, for I knew all this. When first my mother had told me, when I was a boy of ten summers, it had made me hate King Arthur. Perhaps I hated him still, in my bones, but my soul cried out like a prisoner in torment, protesting that a king cannot be held to blame for any bloody act in defense of his throne.

I said to the blind harper, "I have given up trying to change the song's ending. But I would like to save what is left of my soul." The poor, defeated thing.

"See a holy man."

"No." I had no use for pious hermits. "I mean really save it, put it in safekeeping, as the druids used to do for heroes venturing into the realms of the dead. Or so the old tales say."

His fingers stopped strumming at his harp strings and he grew very still. The raven sat on his shoulder, making small croaking noises deep in its black-feathered throat.

"You are of druid blood," I guessed.

"Yes. I can help you. Do you trust me?"

Why should I trust him? I scarcely trusted anyone. All my life I had moved among people like ice floating on the eddies between them, unmoored. Perhaps my mother's witchcraft had chilled me in the womb. Or perhaps it was the long helpless days exposed on the ocean that had made me so cold.

"Your soul must be given to someone you trust," the harper said, "or it will not be given at all."

"Let me think," I told him, and I got up.

"Oddling," the raven accused my back as I walked away.

I walked alone, as the raven had known I must. Indeed I *was* an oddling, a solitary sort of fool, for who would be true to me, whom could I trust?

My friends? I had none. Nor had I any sweetheart.

144

My half-brothers, Gawain, Gaheris, Gareth? No. They smiled on me and humored me as if I were a child and did not truly believe anything I told them.

My guardian, King Lot? He was a man like a stone in a castle wall, strong, enduring, but not one to think or dream. Like his sons, he understood me not at all.

My mother, the sorceress? She understood me well, and I worshipped her for her wisdom and beauty, but no, I did not trust her. In fact I trusted her less than any of the others, for it was she who had set destiny in motion, she who had seduced my father.

My—father . . .

The king.

King Arthur.

How strange—but yes, yes, I would go to him. In all the world he was the only one with whom I felt a kinship, a bond, even though it was an eerie bond made entirely of prophecy, of Merlin's words festering in my blood and bones.

"So, Mordred? What is it? You are unhappy?"

At my request King Arthur had granted me private audience, coming out to walk with me atop Camelot's high walls. As always, he spoke with friendly courtesy. I wanted far more from him. But if he granted me the one thing I would ask today, such useless desire would stop forever.

There was no way to approach the matter delicately, though I tried.

"Sire," I said, "because it was necessary that Jesus our Lord should die, Judas was born. And then after he had done what he was destined to do, he went out into the night and hanged himself."

I think I took his breath away. But he knew at once that I spoke of his own doom, and he did not flinch from it. After a moment he said, "Do not fear hanging, Mordred. I will kill you with the sword if you cross me."

"*If*, Sire? But you know Merlin tells no lies." I was miserable with hating what I was destined to do, and I let him see the misery. "Why have you not killed me already? Why do you not do it now, this very moment? There is no need for the sword. One hard shove and it would be over." The castle wall dropped steeply away below us, three houses tall, to the moat on one side, the hard cobbled yard on the other.

He did not look at me, but stared into the west, and he said, "I was heartsick, last time. I did not want to live my life at such a price. Then I was glad despite all reason when I found that you had survived." And that was the closest he ever came to calling me his son.

We walked in silence, side by side, with the nearly-spoken truth hovering on the air between us, until I could not bear that haunted silence any longer and spoke.

"My king, it is not hanging I fear," I told him, "or death. But until death comes, it is hard for me to be who I am. What I am." I waited for his reply. He gave me none. I said, "Sire, you offered me a boon once. I will claim it now."

"Do not ask me to kill you in cold blood."

"No, Sire. There is a span of life left to me, and I am not so willing to throw it away. But neither do I wish to spend it suffering." Then I stood still, and faced him, and described to him what I wanted him to do for me.

He was so aghast that his gray eyes winced and his face paled behind his beard. "Sir Mordred," he protested.

"Sire, I charge you by your promised boon to do this thing. It is because of you that I find myself born to be in constant pain."

We stood staring at each other, he strong and tall and fair, I thin and dark and vehement. Perhaps as he stood there on the wall with me he tried to see in me something of himself. I am sure he did, and I am sure he failed. I know this because I had so often and always failed, trying to see in myself something of him.

"Sire," I urged.

"You are certain this fearsome thing is what you wish."

"Yes."

"Then I must do as you say."

We had to wait for some days, until the moon had waned and the time for doing magical acts had come. Then when it came, the night of the dark of the moon, we had to wait until innocents were asleep. Long after dark, in the chill of midnight, we assembled far outside the walls of Camelot, on the heath. It was just the three of us: King Arthur, and I, and the blind harper with the raven riding on his shoulder, black and invisible in the black night.

The harper had explained to me what I must do, and I did it. I unlaced my tunic to bare myself. I stood facing the east, with my arms spread wide so as to unlock my chest, with my hands straining back. I stood thus while he chalked the faery circle around all three of us for protection from the spirits of the night. Night is dangerous always, but we

would be especially at its mercy while the spell made us vul-
nerable, while he opened me. He anointed my face and bared
chest and outflung wrists with pungent oil, his blind hands
fumbling at me so that I shuddered. Then he took his place
and struck his harp, and the words he chanted were strange
words in the druidic tongue.

King Arthur faced me, his hands waiting at his heart,
holding open a small silk-lined casket of pure gold to receive
the white moth that would fly from my chest.

It was far easier than it should have been, than it would
have been for anyone with better mooring than I. Without
even a need to say goodbye I felt it fly, I felt it happen, I
felt self take wing. Before, there had been the slow constant
ache of my struggle with fate. As soul took flight there was
a sharper pang, as if my body were a harp string, plucked.
Then there was a simple, welcome nothingness, a soundless
peace, and near my face I saw the white moth fluttering in
the night.

The king awaited it with pale face but steady hands, to
cherish it for my sake. Though to tell the truth, once I was
free of the troublesome thing I no longer cared whether he
cherished it or not. I let my arms fall slack to my sides. The
stillness within me was complete. Nothing mattered to me.
Nothing.

Dancing on the dark air went my soul, no larger than a
dandelion puff, hardly as substantial as cloud wisp, and with
huge relief I watched it go. And then, before it reached the
king, there was a harsh noise I did not at first recognize, and
a clacking sound, and it was gone.

The Raven

The raven! I had given no thought to the raven until it sounded its triumphant croak and moved, black and unseen in the moonless night, and snapped up the tiny white thing. I heard its wings rustle like the devil's black silk robe as it flew away. And I heard its throaty laughter as it flew, and the hoarse words it flung back at me. "Mordred! More dread, more dead, murdered, Mordred!"

King Arthur let the golden casket clatter to the ground and turned toward the harper, saying angrily, "Is this your doing, fellow?"

But the harper was gone. Perhaps he was a demon, and had vanished, a puff of black smoke in the black night. Or perhaps he was merely a prudent man fleeing the king's wrath, a blind man moving more quickly than we sighted ones in the dark. I never knew truly what he was, for I never saw him or heard news of him again.

The king and I found our way back to Camelot in silence. We did not speak until we had reached those torchlit halls, where he stopped me in that orange glow and looked at me. "Sir Mordred?" he asked.

"I am grateful," I told him, and those were the last sincere words I ever spoke to him. Already I felt the old, childish hatred stirring in my blood—now unopposed. No longer would struggle disturb my sleep. "The pain is gone."

"Yes," he said in a low, grim voice, "and so is the light in your eyes."

"It was never of any use to me."

"I had hoped to give your soul back to you someday, some way."

"It does not matter, Sire. I thank you." My thanks were bland. I would be able now to wait in comfort, and eat heartily at his table, and strike him a death blow when it was time. "Nothing matters. Let my soul fly where it will."

"It will be safe enough in that raven, I think." He walked down the shadowy hallway, beckoning me after him. As much to torchlight and shadows as to me he said, "I seem to remember that one of the old gods took the shape of a raven. The druids would invoke its blessing before battle."

Of course. It was the black winged god of bloodshed and carnage and war.

I saw it once more, years later, at the final battle. There on Salisbury Down, as the sun set in a blood-red glow and a hundred thousand men lay dead, as only King Arthur and I and two others were left standing. Then, black out of the sunset, something both eerie and familiar swooped low, laughing its croaking laugh. At that moment, as the black bird passed over us both, King Arthur gave me my mortal wound with his spear. But I welcomed the wound, and ran up the spear, and struck him with my sword through his helmet into his skull.

It is odd, how it has ended. I thought my destiny was to kill us both, but in a sense we have both lived because of what I did. King Arthur did not die of his wound, but sleeps, so people say. He is at Glastonbury, and Cornwall, and Avalon, and everywhere in England, and he will come again when England needs him worst. Even now that hundreds of years have come and gone he is not forgotten.

Even now that hundreds of years have come and gone he is not forgotten.

As for me: I still live, for the old gods do not die. I am the raven, half villain, half holy. I fly over Tower Hill in London, or along the cliffs of Wales, or over the northern heath, or above the ancient circle of Stonehenge. Seeing me, people say I am good luck.

Good luck! I, Mordred the murderer?

Yet perhaps it can be true.

For many years I have harmed no one. I am very old, nearly as ancient as Stonehenge, and therefore somewhat wiser than when I was a man. And now that I am again at one with my soul, I remember how I loved my father Arthur as well as I was able to love anyone. Therefore I stay awake while he sleeps, I guard his land, and await his coming again. And I dream of him often, thinking back on the days when I was a youth and served a great king at Camelot.

Though I do not deserve or expect it, I would very much like to be born as his true son next time. Above all I would like to look at him with my love lighting my eyes—and smile.

King Arthur, with his customary valor, led squadron after squadron of cavalry into the attack and Sir Mordred encountered him unflinchingly. As the number of dead and wounded mounted on both sides, the active combatants continued dauntless until nightfall, when four men alone survived.

from *Le Morte d'Arthur* by
Sir Thomas Malory

All the Iron
of Heaven

Mark W. Tiedemann

This can't be Camlatt, Gadis thought, and glanced back down the road toward the hills of Dumnonia.

The place was a fort like many others. Stone and earth foundations, heavy oak walls and turrets. Tents, wattle houses, sod huts collected around it, giving off steam and a hundred different smells. Gadis sighed and wondered if his brother had felt the same coming here two years ago.

Few people were on the road. The faces Gadis saw were all gloomy, like the day, like the world. Perhaps this *was* Camlatt. The King was dead. A week had past already since the battle at Camlan; despair traveled faster than the news. It did not matter that one appointed by Arthur now sat on the throne; it was not Arthur.

Gadis adjusted his bundle on his left shoulder, drew a deep breath, and walked toward the gates.

The guards were playing a half-hearted game of sticks and paid no attention to him. He walked through the gate into the fort unchallenged.

To the left and right were ramparts built up against the stone walls and topped with wooden planks. Just behind these stood thatch-roofed garrison halls for the soldiers. Axes and pikes leaned against the walls. Gadis saw only a few soldiers on the ramparts; one sitting in the doorway of the lefthand hall was absently carving a piece of wood. The smell of burnt meat and a heady barley broth caught his attention; he ran the tip of his tongue over his lower lip. It had been more than a day since his last meal.

Ahead, at the end of a stone street lined with the stalls of merchants and craftsmen, was a tower of massive stones that had been cut and stacked to make a thick blunt finger rising high above the city. Gadis counted four levels at least, judging by the narrow windows. On the top he saw the famous firepot. The beacon was unlit.

As he walked the gauntlet of hawkers toward the tower, they spoke in his own northern tongue, the brutal variants of western and northern Brits, as well as many languages Gadis had never heard. He did not understand any of them in the moil of words; he had never felt so isolated among so many.

A pair of menhirs stood at the end of the road. Beyond the cobblestones gave way to flagged stones. Gadis stopped at the threshold. A few armed men were within the circle surrounding the tower. To the right was a long crude building marked by a Christian cross; to the left a more solid, older hall, with a red dragon emblazoned above the door.

"You have business here?"

Gadis jerked around, startled by the deep, loud voice. A man not much taller than him but heavier, his face darker, bearded, and much rougher than his voice, stood close. Gadis stepped back and glanced down.

A shortsword hung loosely in the man's right hand. He was barefoot; a soiled kilt, the pattern long-since obscured by grime and wear, covered his thighs; a leather vest was tied across a chest matted with reddish-brown hair.

"Ah—" Gadis said. He closed his mouth, swallowed, and tried again. "I, uh—"

"Hm."

"I come to see the king," Gadis said.

The man looked amused for a moment, then shook his head. "I would advise against it. Cador's not kind."

Gadis nodded. He felt himself blushing. He hated losing his words, stumbling over his meaning. It made him feel like a child all over again.

"Still," he said. "I come to find my brother."

The man's eyebrows rose slightly. He stepped closer to Gadis. "Eh? Brother? Why would you come to Camlatt to find your brother?"

Gadis tightened his grip on his bundle and willed himself not to step back. He did anyway. "He came here two years ago, to be a warrior with Arthur. We haven't heard anything since."

"What's your name?"

"Gadis."

"And your brother's?"

"Feric."

Gadis was not sure he heard the man sigh—it might have been a breeze—but something softened in his face.

"Have you eaten?"

"Not in a while."

The man motioned for him to follow him to the dragon hall.

"Sir," Gadis said, "what's your name?"

"Bors. Come on. You better not face Cador on an empty stomach."

Tall, narrow windows let in some light that mingled unpleasantly with the orange glow from the central hearth. A broken circle of tables ranged round the hearth. Gadis made out the shadows of men sitting listlessly at some of the tables, a small group sitting beside the fire. It gave the hall the feel of a game in the middle of play.

Bors led him to a table far from the opposite end of the hall where Gadis saw a large chair with a high back and thick arms. It was unoccupied now, and Gadis felt his heart thump unexpectedly.

He turned to where Bors directed him and sat down. Glancing to his right, he saw a woman in a plain dress working on the leather jerkin of a sleeping man. She looked up for a moment, smiled tentatively, then looked back at her work.

The hall smelled of rotten chicken and sweat.

Bors went to the hearth, spoke quietly to the men seated there, and pulled one of the spits away from the fire. He picked up a wooden bowl and cut some meat from the carcass, then returned to Gadis. The meat was crisped on the surface and smelled so much of smoke, Gadis could not tell what it was.

Bors sat down and watched him eat.

It was fox.

Bors nodded suddenly. "You look like Feric."

Holding his breath, Gadis waited for Bors to continue.

A heavy door slammed in the back of the hall and several people entered. Gadis looked up and saw a small entourage converging on the throne.

A tall man sat on the seat. He wore a plain white kilt and nothing else. His hair was light brown and long and, though thin, he seemed strong, his muscles all defined and gleaming in the orange light.

Two of the men with him were warriors, one with a heavy sword, the other with an axe at his belt; a third, in his long, pale robe and holding an oak staff, had the look of a druid about him; the fourth stood well away from the others, on the other side of the throne, and wore the simple dark brown robes of a monk.

"If I find her," the man on the throne announced, "I will kill her. If I find that anyone has helped her hide from me, I will kill him, too."

Bors grunted softly. "He says that every time he sits on the throne." He looked at Gadis. "The queen. He means the queen." He frowned. "What stories have you heard where you come from? Feric was from the north, wasn't he? Place called . . . Cylanog Fawr, wasn't it? Long way from Camlatt. Longer way from Camlan. What have you heard?"

"I was on my way here when the battle was fought," Gadis said. He stared at the meat; he felt small and lost, a little sick. "Don't know what home has heard." He swallowed drily and looked for something to drink. There was nothing. He coughed and continued. "On the road I heard some say ten thousand died. Others a hundred times that."

Bors watched him intently. "So. You know your brother died, then. I'm sorry."

Gadis shuddered and looked at the meat before him. Feric's death was still unreal to him. He did not want to acknowledge it.

"Who is your guest, Bors?"

Gadis looked up. Cador was standing right before him, staring at him. This close, Cador was difficult to look at. His grey eyes bulged slightly, giving him a mad expression. He held a gold cup in his left hand.

"This is Gadis," Bors said. "Brother of Feric, from the northlands."

"North," Cador said. "But not so far that you come from beyond Logris."

"No, lord," Gadis said.

"No. Logris is a big place. Arthur saw to that." He drank from the cup. "Why are you here?"

"My family sent me to find Feric," Gadis said. "We hadn't heard from him in . . . a long time."

"He's dead."

Gadis looked straight at Cador, startled by his sudden anger. Cador's eyes bulged just a bit more and the beginning of a smile tugged at his mouth.

"You don't like that," he said. "Your brother is dead. At Camlan, with Arthur and all the other heroes. Arthur is dead. Logris is a big place, but now Arthur is dead and it won't be big for long. He gave it to me to hold it together." Cador squatted down to meet Gadis's eyes evenly. "He said, 'Take what's left, hold what you can, do your best.' That's what he said. Oh, and 'God speed you on your way.' Then he died. And every day I have to learn a little more just how impossible a job he gave me. Every day I watch a little more of the realm crack and splinter off, killing the rest bit by bit. I warrant it's at least as hard for me to watch that and know there's nothing I can do about it as it is for you to believe that your brother is truly dead."

"Lord Cador . . ." Bors said quietly.

Cador straightened. "What else did you come here for, Gadis? People come to Camlatt for more than just finding a brother."

Gadis frowned and looked at Bors. He was confused and a little frightened by Cador. It was easy seeing Cador to believe that Arthur was dead. The king would never leave such a man on the throne if he were alive.

"Tell me, boy," Cador said. He rapped his knuckles on the table. "Don't look at Bors, I'm talking to you. Did you come hoping to be one of Arthur's warriors? An equite, maybe? A Roman knight? You look a lot like your brother."

"Yes, sir," Gadis said, wondering what he had just answered.

Cador grinned. "He wants to be a warrior, Bors."

"Lord—" Bors started to stand.

"No." Cador glared at Bors. "No, I think it's a good idea. We *are* short of men these days. I think he should learn from the best, too." He reached to his belt and quickly pulled a long knife. Gadis jumped. Cador extended it toward him. "Touch it."

Gadis put two fingertips to the blade, hesitant and nervous. Cador jerked the knife up and back. The edge bit Gadis's fingers and he pulled back and curled his hand into a fist. When he opened it he saw blood.

"By my iron, name, and spirit," Cador said, "you are now pledged to the realm of Logris." He smiled thinly. "Your first step to being a true equite."

Bors took his hand and dipped his bleeding fingers into a wooden cup of wine. Gadis sucked his breath through his teeth and tried to pull away, but Bors's grip was unbreakable. Finally Bors let him go and set the cup before him.

"Your first task," Cador said, "is to accompany Bors. He'll teach you what you need to know. You're in *his* service until he—or I—say otherwise." He turned and went back to the throne.

Gadis picked up the cup and drank. His fingers throbbed.

"I should have known better," Bors said.

"I—don't be sorry. It's what I want. In part."

Bors shook his head. "It's not any part of what you want, boy. Believe me." He stood. "Come on. I'll get you ready to come with me."

"Where are we going?"

"Your first quest in the service of the king. We're going to Camlan."

•   ♦   ♦

Bors rode a large black mare. Gadis walked beside him, carrying a heavy pack and a pike. Behind them rode a few other knights, all surly and untalkative, and behind them a column of soldiers—mostly Scotti mercenaries—and workmen, Saxon prisoners and beggars.

Bors said little. He watched the forest and the hills, eyes never resting, and glanced at the men at his back more than a few times with an uneasy squint.

After walking from sunrise to dusk, Gadis had to gather wood, make a fire, prepare the bedding for both Bors and himself. He ate a little smoked lamb, and went to sleep. It was three days' travel to Camlan. He was too tired to talk at night, too nervous to break Bors's watchful silence during the day.

The morning of the third day he could smell the battlefield. The odor was sickly sweet, filling the air with a cloying sourness. At first he pulled at the scent, curious about it, but by midday he wished he could filter it somehow, ignore it. The others wore expressions he was certain he mirrored.

Bors sniffed a few times now and then, but did not seem to care.

A wall of black smoke rose over the horizon. The stench of burnt flesh emerged, became as strong as the other, uglier smell. *If a foul belly had an odor,* Gadis thought, *this would be it.*

They crested a low hill just before dusk and stopped.

Stretching to the distant treeline at the foot of the next row of hills was the field of Camlan. The low sun caught the sheen of iron, colored the earth and flesh amber and sienna, smeared the clumps of bodies and gouges of dirt into a single object. The light rippled through the layers of smoke rising above the field.

There was movement. Scattered piles of smoldering fires were tended by people wrapped head to foot in grey and brown. In pairs they carried bodies to the nearest pyre and tossed them on.

Bors moved along, toward an encampment overlooking the field. Following, Gadis kept staring at the valley, amazed.

A tall man with black hair and pale eyes stood before the largest tent, his hands on his hips. Bors dismounted and handed the reins to Gadis.

"Rhafid." Bors clasped the man's hand.

"You're late," the man called Rhafid said.

Bors glanced back at his column and shook his head. "It was hard to get them to come. Cador had to threaten some of them."

"Cador." Rhafid sighed. "I don't know if I'd rather stay here with the bodies or go home to the corpse." He grunted. "Come on. There's a good stew."

"Let me get my men settled," Bors said. "Then I'll have a bowl."

Rhafid nodded and turned away, entering the tent.

Gadis could not smell any stew. All he smelled was the field, the metallic tang of iron and blood.

Bors took the reins back.

"This is the part no one tells you about," Bors said. "The bards, the princes, they all speak of the glory of battle, the shouting, the fever of a hatred that has no name, the moment it turns for you and triumph carries your soul to the edge of heaven. They never tell you of this."

Gadis did not know what to say. He hoped Bors did not expect him to go down onto Camlan, among the dead.

"You came looking for your brother," Bors said. "He's out there somewhere. Along with the king and hundreds of others." Gadis gave him a startled look and Bors nodded. "That's right. We never found Arthur's body. Not that we could tell, anyway. I'm sure some think he's still alive."

Bors led his horse away. After a few minutes, Gadis followed.

The campfires helped hide Camlan. Gadis huddled close to the fire round which Bors's warriors' servants grouped to eat and drink and tell stories. For the most part they spoke of Camlan or Camlatt. A few had been in Camlatt when Cador had returned with the standard and the mandate from Arthur.

Gadis listened to the descriptions of the ashen-faced warriors coming through the gates in a loose line, dispirited and broken; how Cador had stayed in the tower chambers of the king for two days before emerging to announce that Camlan should be cleaned up and that the queen, Guineva, was to be found and brought to him for judgment of her crimes with Mordred; how many of the surviving warriors left, in anger or despair, to find some other place, to live some other life.

Gadis listened until he started to fall asleep. Then he left the fire and walked off into the dark to relieve himself. Blinking his eyes, he looked up, and realized he was at the edge of the ridge, looking out over Camlan.

The several pyres smoldered with a dim, reddish glow. Clouds had moved overhead, blotting out the stars. Behind him faint voices mingled with the crackle of the fires. Gadis imagined himself trapped between the two worlds, caught in transition from one to the next. *Odd,* he thought, *how both are marked by fire.*

He shuddered and twisted his head down and away to break the hold of his imagination. When he looked back at Camlan he saw the cometglows of torches on the far end, moving slowly through the darkness.

He stepped backward, his heel catching on something, and he sat down, hard. His heart hammered. Fear dulled his thoughts and he watched the torches for a long time. There were five of them and they moved methodically, pausing after each short transit. Gadis did not want to know what they were, even while part of him demanded he find out. He remained there, unable to move. Eventually the torches went away.

In the morning he awoke and saw men and boys wrapping themselves in shrouds, like corpses. They wrapped their hands and feet in strips of linen and tied masks over their lower faces. For a moment he believed he was still dreaming. Then he saw Bors coming toward him.

"Come on," Bors said. "I'll show you how to do this. The stench is foul enough here but down there . . . well, this helps."

Gadis shook his head. "I'm not going down."

Bors frowned. "What did you say?"

"I'm not going down." Gadis looked over his shoulder at the mist-covered field. "There's spirits."

Bors grabbed him by the shirt. He brought Gadis close to his face and whispered tightly, "Quiet. I've got trouble enough with this bunch of Scotti idiots. Now wrap up and be still." He shoved Gadis back. "You came to find your brother. This is the only chance you've got."

Gadis clenched his fists. "He might be burned already!"

Bors snapped his hand up and Gadis flinched, but the blow never fell. Lowering his hand, Bors stepped back.

"I've never struck a man I wasn't prepared to kill," Bors said. "I'm sorry. Now—*please*—wrap up and help."

Gadis felt embarrassed for the warrior. He did not know how to accept the apology and knew he was blushing. He looked away.

"Last night," he said, not looking at Bors, "I saw spirits moving away on the other side. I saw their lights, saw them go from man to man to take his soul." Gadis knew he sounded foolish, but he wanted to give Bors some of his dignity back and thought this would be enough. Hesitantly, he looked at Bors and saw the man staring past him across the field.

"Don't say anything about that to the others," Bors said. "Not a word. Hear me?"

Gadis nodded.

"Those . . . spirits . . . won't hurt you," Bors said. "Believe me. Now come on. There's work to do."

◆　◆　◆

Gadis had never had such a day. The mist burned off just as they stepped onto Camlan field. At his feet he saw a severed arm, greyed and encrusted with dried blood and dirt. He squeezed his eyes shut until he could control his shaking, then carefully looked at the far line of trees and walked into the field. He did it for Bors, for the shame he had caused the warrior, for the chance that he might find his brother, for scores of reasons he called to mind and repeated to himself to dull the things immediately before him.

Going from place to place, Gadis lifted body after body, part after part, and helped carry the scattered fragments of combat to the pyres. His thoughts became a drone inside his head, counting the trips back and forth. When the others stopped to eat and drink, he walked away and found a fairly clear space, sat down, and wept to the sky. Bors found him and brought him back to the task and he worked the balance of the day in a mental fog.

In his village there had always been someone—an old man or a wandering bard or a stranger passing through—who spoke of war in glorious terms. By the end of the day Gadis knew all such men were liars.

He opened his eyes at the touch of a hand on his shoulder. Bors was kneeling beside him, his face dimly outlined by a campfire. He pointed out at the field.

The torches were there again.

"Spirits," Gadis breathed.

"No," Bors said. "Not spirits. Come on. Here." He shoved an axe into Gadis's hands and stood.

His heart stuttering in fear, Gadis followed down the

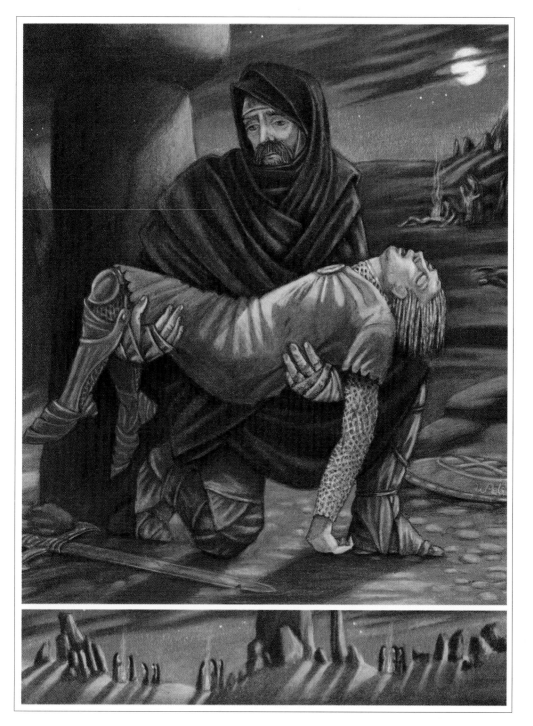

*Gadis lifted body after body, part after part, and helped carry
the scattered fragments of combat to the pyres.*

slope. He loped alongside Bors across the sullen ground. The dying glow of the pyres marked their way.

Bors slowed as they neared the far side. He laid a hand on Gadis's shoulder and pushed him into a crouch, then crept forward. Gadis could hear the sounds of people moving and whispering among themselves.

They rounded a pyre and Gadis jumped to see the spirits so close.

There was a woman in a dark dress with gold around her neck and on her wrists kneeling beside a corpse. Around her were two more women in plainer clothes and two men, one old, the other young and armed with a broadsword. The four held torches high, the old man holding two.

The kneeling woman rose then and took the second torch from the old man and they all moved toward another body.

Bors had stopped just beyond the circle of light cast by the torches. Gadis moved closer to him.

"Who?" he asked.

"The queen," Bors whispered. "Guineva."

"They took him, my lady," one of the women said. "He's gone now. Gone to the island."

"Hush," the old man said.

Guineva knelt beside another body. She looked intently into the face of the dead soldier, then stood and went to another.

Bors straightened and started to turn. Suddenly a clatter of iron broke the quiet.

The young warrior turned, raising his sword. Four armed men erupted from the darkness.

Bors rushed toward them, bellowing in rage.

When the attackers saw him, they hesitated and Bors ran between them to the queen's entourage.

Gadis stepped forward, holding the axe awkwardly. He recognized the four men from the camp—Scotti mercenaries. They glowered at Bors, their swords held before them, not quite pointed at Bors.

"Go back to camp!" Bors bellowed. "You've no concerns here!"

One of the men gestured toward Guineva. "Cador wants her dead. There's a price for her."

"Cador doesn't have the money to pay you," Bors said. "I said go back to camp."

"Cador can pay us to pick up the dead, he can pay us for one more body," the man said. "Who's going to say no to us?"

Bors raised his sword. "It would be a mistake on your part."

Gadis entered the light of the torches. The four mercenaries glanced at him. The queen's warrior, hefting his broadsword, stepped closer to Bors's flank.

"There's three of us," Bors said quietly to the Scotti. "And two of us survived Camlan. What have you four done recently to recommend you?"

Gadis felt his legs weaken. Standing beside Bors, he held onto the axe, praying he could stand in a fight.

The four Scotti glanced at each other. The one who had spoken grimaced. He started to turn away, then suddenly lunged.

Bors brushed the man's sword aside, spun smoothly around, and rammed his elbow into the mercenary's face. The man dropped and Bors continued his turn, gripping his sword with both hands, swinging the blade into the neck of the next man.

The other two ran off into the night.

"Thank you, Bors."

Guineva stood close to the tall warrior. Gadis saw that her face was lined and smudged. Her eyes, in the torchlight, seemed to be black holes in her thin face.

Bors bowed his head briefly. He did not look happy.

"My lady," Bors said. "I was sent here to clean up the mess we left. I don't remember Cador saying anything about bounty hunting."

Guineva frowned slightly, then nodded. "The other two may still be out there."

Bors looked at Gadis. "Go with her. See she gets safely back to her camp." He looked at the queen's warrior. "You won't mind the company, will you, Lance?"

Guineva raised her eyebrows at Gadis, then smiled wryly. "So much for old friendships. Still . . ."

"I can defend the queen," Lance said.

"I'm sure," Bors said. "But I'd as soon take no chances. Take Gadis with you. An extra arm can't hurt."

Guineva stepped around Bors and walked off. The others fell in behind her.

"Sir?" Gadis said.

"Don't worry," Bors said. "Those other two will be halfway to Pictland by morning. And the queen doesn't bite." He grunted. "I have to make sure the rest of the men are still in camp. Come back in the morning."

Bors walked away. Gadis sighed and hurried after Guineva.

He stayed on the opposite side of the group from Lance, who glared at him a couple of times, then ignored him. When they entered the woods, animals scurrying for cover caused Gadis to jump at every sound.

Guineva walked with her head erect, proudly. Gadis kept staring at her, certain that this, too, was a dream. He wondered why anyone would want to kill her.

A twig snapped. Gadis heard a sound like wind, then a wet thud. Everyone stopped.

Lance raised his sword and one of the mercenaries backed away from him. A patch of dark moisture spread over Lance's stomach.

Dry leaves crackled quietly behind Gadis, and, unthinking, he spun round, swung the axe up. A sword glanced off its blade. In the harsh yellow light of the torch, he could not see the mercenary's eyes, only shadows above high cheekbones, and big, crooked teeth. The man twisted at the waist, bringing his sword back.

Terrified, Gadis charged, slammed into the mercenary, and they fell. Something wet splashed his face, he felt warm breath that smelled foul. He scrambled to stand and tried to pick up the axe. It was stuck.

He backed away, staring down at the dead man. The axe was deep in his chest. Wiping his fingers across his cheek, Gadis looked at them. The blood was nearly black in the torchglow.

His breath came faster, almost too heavy to stand. He

turned to tell someone that he had just killed a man. But everyone was huddled around Lance, who lay stretched out on the ground. His chest heaved unevenly, his breath a ragged gasp. Guineva held his hand.

A short distance away was the body of the other mercenary.

Gadis needed to say what he had just done. He tried to speak, but only sobbed.

The old man looked at him curiously, then came over to him. Glancing at the mercenary with the axe in his chest, he nodded.

"You've done well, boy," he said. "You've defended the queen. You should be proud."

Gadis looked at the old man and suddenly his breath calmed. He saw a kind of wisdom in the old man's face, and the illusion that this was someone he could trust. But the words the man spoke did not match his face.

"My brother died at Camlan," Gadis said finally.

The old man seemed to think about that for a moment, then nodded again. "You come from a brave family. You deserve to be proud. Of him and yourself."

Gadis bit his lip to keep silent. The old man was saying nothing real, only lies matched to illusions. He remembered his mother saying to him that when everything else failed he could call to heaven for the iron to protect himself. "I have no more use for such illusions," he muttered.

"What?" the old man asked, frowning.

Gadis stepped away from the old man's reach. Pulling the axe from the corpse, he walked away. He thought he heard someone call after him, but it might have been the wind. He ignored the sound and crossed Camlan.

In the morning he was far away from the battlefield. He did not look back.

Afterward, he never listened to anyone who told stories about Camlatt. He never listened to old men who had forgotten what war really was.

When news of King Arthur's death reached Queen Gwynevere in the Tower of London, she renounced all her worldly estates, and with five of her ladies entered the abbey of Amesbury. There she became abbess and, adopting the white-and-black cloth of the order, with fasting and prayer sought atonement for her long years of vain and carnal sin. And so great was the change wrought in her person by her repentance that all who witnessed it marveled.

from *Le Morte d'Arthur* by
Sir Thomas Malory

Amesbury Song

Jane Yolen

Adam Stemple

Refrain
Plaintively

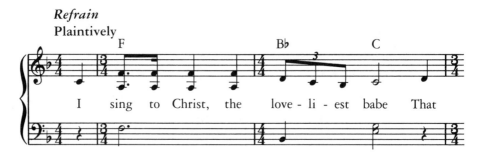

I sing to Christ, the love - li - est babe That

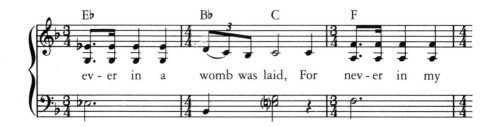

ev - er in a womb was laid, For nev - er in my

Fine

womb shall be A child to grace e - ter - ni - ty.

1. A___ maid came I from my fa - ther's

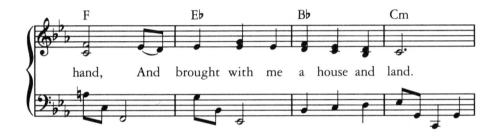

hand, And brought with me a house and land.

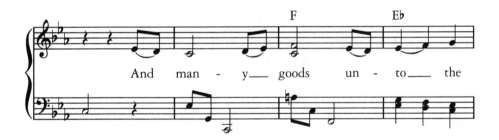

And man - y___ goods un - to___ the

D.C. al Fine

throne, But nev - er a maid did I___ go home.

Refrain

I sing to Christ, the loveliest babe
That ever in a womb was laid,
For never in my womb shall be
A child to grace eternity.

Verses

1. A maid came I from my father's hand,
   And brought with me a house and land
   And many goods unto the throne,
   But never a maid did I go home.

2. A wife came I to my husband's bed,
   Who took from me my maidenhead.
   But lay I then far from the throne
   And never a good wife did I go home.

3. A queen came I to Camelot
   Where I was queen and then was not,
   And loved the king but not the throne,
   And never as queen did I go home.

4. A nun came I to Amesbury
   And brought my shame and joy with me.
   And till I kneel before the throne
   Of God, this cell shall be my home.

   I sing to Christ, the loveliest babe
   That ever in a womb was laid,
   For never in my womb shall be
   A child to grace eternity.

178

In many parts of Britain it is believed that
King Arthur did not die and that he will return to us and win fresh glory . . . but for
myself I do not believe this, and would leave
him buried peacefully in his tomb at Glastonbury, where the Archbishop of Canterbury
and Sir Bedivere humbled themselves, and
with prayers and fasting honored his memory.
And enscribed on his tomb, men say, is this
legend:

HIC JACET ARTHURUS,
REX QUONDAM REXQUE FUTURUS
(Here lies Arthur, the once and future king)

from *Le Morte d'Arthur* by
Sir Thomas Malory

Our Hour of Need

Greg Costikyan

"Sir Kay's horn sounds," Don said, "a final time. And then his standard wavers and falls."

For a long moment, none of us could speak. I fiddled with the twenty-sided die. "Then we are done for," said Karen.

José was obviously upset. "Nay, my lady," he said fiercely. "So long as life breathes through our bodies, our cause is not yet lost."

"The Saxon line is readying for another charge," said Don warningly.

"Sir Trenus," I told José, "we are o'ermatched. We cannot hope to hold. If we wish to further serve our cause, we must withdraw."

"Abandon Norgales to the foe?" he said incredulously.

"Too many knights have fallen this day," Martin said. "Would you join them?"

José sighed. "Everyone think we ought to go?" he said.

Karen nodded. Rupert whined and thumped his tail once; perhaps he heard the stress in our voices.

"Veillantif neighs agreement," Don said. We all smiled, the tension broken. My dog had seemed to want to play in on our game from the start, so Don had assigned him an appropriate role—as my character's horse.

"Then I will stay," José said, "to cover your retreat."

"No, Sir Trenus," I said. "Without you, we cannot . . ."

"Someone must," he said. "Look! The Saxons are gathering once more."

"He's right," Don said.

José turned to Martin. "Good priest," he said. "I would confess before you go."

Martin nodded gravely, and the two went into the dining room to speak for a few moments.

"So we leave," Karen told Don.

"And in the distance," said Don, "you hear the renewed sounds of battle as your destriers eat the ground between Norgales and Mount Snowdon."

José and Martin returned from their conference. "What happens to me?" said José.

"Care to roll some dice to see how many Saxons you kill before you're slain?"

José waved a hand. "Not really," he said.

"Okay," said Don.

We were all silent again for a moment.

"This," Karen told Don, "is a bummer."

Don shrugged. "So you guys said you were tired of killing monsters. I told you this was going to be a tragedy. You said you thought it would be interesting."

"Then I will stay," José said, "to cover your retreat."

"Don't get me wrong," Karen said. "It's interesting. I'm just not sure it's fun."

"Want to quit?" Don said.

"No way," Karen said.

Don smiled.

"Okay," I said. "So Wales is all that's left of Arthur's realm?"

"The pagans have Sugales," he reminded me.

"Not even all of Wales," I said. "And we've got no army left to speak of. Does anyone see *anything* we can do?"

Karen shook her head.

Don looked around the table. "Nothing?" he said.

We all looked at him.

"Nothing?" he repeated.

"Are we being obtuse?" said Martin.

"Perhaps you ought to pray for guidance," said Don.

"Fine," said Martin.

"And in your prayers, you receive a vision. A vision of a boat, floating across the Severn Sea, moved by no power known to man. And in the boat, lying in his bier, is . . ."

"Arthur Pendragon," said Martin.

Don smiled.

"Who shall return," said Martin with increasing excitement, "in Britain's hour of need."

"Damn . . ." said José softly.

"And God knows we need him now," I said.

"We must go," said Karen, "to the Severn coast, and there implore almighty God to return our king . . ."

". . . that Britain may be saved," I said. We smiled at each other.

183

"Good," said Don briskly. "This is going to be the culmination of the campaign. So I want to do it a little differently. I want you to meet me at the beach at midnight tonight."

"Midnight?" Karen said uncertainly. "If my folks find out . . ."

"C'mon, you can sneak out," he said. "What's the problem?"

Karen sighed. "All right, Don," she said. "But if I get caught, I'll tell 'em it's your fault."

Don shrugged.

"Where should we meet?" I asked.

"Why not in front of your house, Sarah?" he said. "It's on the beach and pretty central."

"Fine by me," I said.

José and I biked back to the beach. Rupert trotted alongside, occasionally foraying into the bushes after imaginary rabbits. José's folks had a house on the water, too, about a mile up the beach road from mine. "The Kennedys used to come here, you know," he said.

"Of course I know that, José," I said. It seemed to be one of Hyannis Port's main attractions for tourists. There were signs all over the place. It was hard to miss.

José blushed and swerved to miss a puddle. "They called it Camelot, too," he said.

"Who called what?" I said.

"In the sixties," he said. "JFK's administration. You ever read *The Best and the Brightest*?"

"No," I said.

"We had it in history," he said. "Kennedy brought in all these intellectuals."

"You mean," I said, "he assembled the great knights of the realm at his castle in . . ."

"Washington," he said. "And he did unify the land to fight the pagan foe . . ."

"The Russians," I said. "And he ruled wisely and well, until he was betrayed . . ."

"By a lone assassin on a grassy knoll." José laughed.

"Right," I said, grinning. We rode on for a moment. "Do you think that's why Don chose King Arthur?"

"You mean the Camelot association? And because his dad is active in Democratic politics?"

"Yeah," I said.

José shrugged. "Maybe," he said. "I think he'd just been reading T. H. White and was tired of playing *Dungeons & Dragons.* He wanted something different."

"Well," I said. "We sure got it. I'm sorry you died, José."

"That's okay," he said.

"But you invested a lot of time in Sir Trenus."

"Yeah, I guess I did," he said. "How long have we been playing now?"

"Two months," I said. "Twice a week."

A bus passed and we couldn't talk for a while over the noise. We came to the beach road and we both stopped. José had to go east here, and I west. He stood over his bike with one foot on the ground and looked out at all the lotion-oiled people on the beach. "So I died," he said. "This is tragedy;

185

everyone's supposed to die." He smiled at me. "At least I died a glorious death."

"You going to be at the beach tonight? Even though you're dead?"

"Of course," he said. "I wouldn't miss it. Suppose Arthur answers our call?"

I smiled. "Then the story would have a happy ending, wouldn't it?" I said. "You don't think Don's going to let that happen, do you?"

José laughed. "You never can tell," he said. "See you tonight, Sarah."

He pedalled down the road. Rupert wanted to run after José, and I had to whistle to bring him back.

Dad was sitting in the living room when I got home. That was odd. It was Wednesday; Dad had to work. Normally, he only got out to the Cape on weekends. I gave him a hug and sat down on the couch.

It was unusual for Dad to be watching TV. Normally, he wouldn't even watch the TV news, and he always sort of gave me a glare when I wanted to watch. But he had the news on now. He was looking worried.

"Have you heard?" he said.

"What?"

"The President's put the armed forces on Red Alert."

That put a chill down my spine. "What for?" I said.

"They're worried about the Soviet situation," he said.

Sure enough, some talking head on the TV was babbling about the negotiations in Geneva. ". . . reported to be at loggerheads. The State Department released a statement re- porting no progress in today's talks. Meanwhile, unsubstanti- ated rumors in Washington say that CIA satellite photography show that Soviet reserves are mobilizing all across the Ukraine and Byelorussia . . ."

"Could this be it?" I said.

Dad looked at me soberly. "It could," he said. "That's why I'm here. I suspect fallout patterns would affect the Cape . . . but if anything happens, I want to be with you and your mother."

"You're serious, aren't you?" I said, a little frightened.

Dad sighed. "It's probably a false alarm," he said. "There's been the threat of nuclear war longer than I've been alive. We really thought Gorbachev was going to change things, but now that those hard-liners are in power . . ." He shook his head.

We sat and listened to the TV for a while. Then a Chevro- let commercial came on. "You know," Dad said, "some- thing's gone out of this country since I was a kid."

"What's that?" I said.

"We used to be pretty optimistic," he said. "I remember the Kennedy Administration. I was a kid then but America was on top of the world, every problem was solvable. Now, it's like we're not only in decline, but resigned to decline. All our problems seem intractable, so we do our best to ig- nore them. And you never see smiling faces on the street anymore."

"Is it really that bad?"

He looked at me and smiled. "Maybe not," he said. "I

can imagine my grandfather saying the same thing. 'Things just ain't been the same since Teddy Roosevelt was president, by cracky.' Maybe I'm getting old."

"Boy," I said. "This has been a pretty depressing day."

"What else happened?" he said, frowning.

"The Saxons took Norgales," I said.

He laughed. "They did, did they? Where's that?"

"Lancashire," I said. "The part of England right north of Wales."

"Oh," he said. "You guys aren't doing too well, are you?"

"We're doing the best we can," I said. "It's just—we're supposed to lose. Don set it up as a tragedy, so the best we can do is stave off the end."

The talking heads were back on the TV. Dad raised an eyebrow. "Maybe that's the best anyone can do," he muttered.

Mom lit Sabbath candles that night. She hadn't done that in a long time. I guess she felt as nervous as Dad.

Every time a plane flew overhead, I strained, listening. If it were a Soviet bomber, I'd hear a sonic boom, wouldn't I? Or maybe their bombers weren't supersonic, like the old B-52's. Or actually, they'd use missiles, right? I guess you wouldn't hear anything until the nuke went off.

Finally, I got up and went down to the beach. Rupert came along. I sat on the sand and looked out; Rupert hunkered down and leaned against me. The moon was almost full; its light tipped the breakers with silver, and the susurrus of the waves made a gentle rhythm. The stars were brilliant, even with the moon out. Used to Boston's skies, I was always amazed by how bright the stars were on Cape Cod. I wished José were with me; he knows lots of the constellations.

A spark streaked across the sky; I held my breath. It was a shooting star. There was another one, west and fainter; I kept on looking. There were lots of them. José once told me that late August is meteor season. The remnants of a comet intersect Earth's orbit. On the right nights, you can see dozens of shooting stars.

It was beautiful.

The first to show up was Martin. He'd found two pieces of driftwood, and had nailed them into a cross. "Godspeed," he said.

"And to you, Abbot Mortain," I said.

He stabbed the cross into the sand and sat down not too far away. "What do you think is going to happen?" he asked. He took a crushed paper cup someone had left on the beach and used it to scoop out a narrow trench.

"He's not going to come," I said. "No way Don's going to give us a happy ending."

"And yet," Martin said, straightening a little, "God has granted me a vision."

"Aye, good Abbot," I said. "Surely our King will return in Britain's hour of need. And surely it seems to us that this hour is nigh. Yet we are mortal; we can escry but a tiny corner of God's plan. Who can say if this is Britain's direst hour? Your vision promises us Arthur's return—but now?

Or centuries, millennia hence? The Lord means to comfort us—but comfort us, perhaps, only in our loss. Mayhap no promise of aid is meant."

"Well spoken," said Don from behind us. Karen was with him. With a little shock, I realized they were holding hands. Karen and I were best friends, but I'd never realized . . .

José came flying down the beach and plunged into the sand next to me. "Am I too late?" he asked.

"We're just about to start," said Don. "Who wants to go first?"

Martin stood up and took the staff of his cross in one hand. He looked out over the sea. "O Lord our God," he said. "In this hour of dire peril, we turn to thee. Arthur's realm lies prostrate before the Saxon foe. Our cities are in ruins, our armies scattered before the winds. We beg of thee, lend us aid in our time of need."

Karen walked up and stood next to Martin. "Jesus Christ," she said, "whose blood was shed for all humanity; hear us now. Rome is fallen and Europe enslaved. Here on the Severn shore are gathered all that remains of civilization, the last flame of learning flickering before the gathering storm. Can it be God's plan that this flame should die? This is Britain's hour of need. This is civilization's hour of need. This is Rome's final hour. Succor us, we implore thee."

Rupert went wild. He darted up the beach, tail wagging. Dad was walking toward us.

"What's up, kids?" he said. I guess he'd woken up and seen us out the window.

"Uh, gee, Dad," I said. "We . . . we're playing the game."

"Isn't it a little late?"

"This is the end of the campaign," Don said. "I wanted something special . . ."

Dad sighed. "No harm done, I guess," he said. He looked as if he'd gotten as little sleep as I.

"It's your turn, Sarah," said Don. So I went and stood by Karen.

"Holy Spirit," I said, "that doth live within us. We have lost our lands, our families, our future. All that remains is loyalty: to our God and King. Our hopes are shattered, and yet still we hope. Send us our King! Let him renew us and lead us: lead us not to bloody victory over the foe, but to peace. For well we know that Saxons have souls, and 'tis better to bring them to the glory of God than to slay them in battle. Let the Lord's peace spread over Britain; over Europe; over all the world. Send us peace; send us hope; send us Arthur."

We stood silently for a moment. Then, Martin—rather, Abbot Mortain, our man of God—said "Kyrie eleison."

"Christe eleison," we said. Don didn't join in—he was the gamemaster, not a character—but José did; I remembered that he was Catholic.

"Kyrie eleison."

"Christe eleison."

"Gloria in excelsis Deo," said Martin, "et in terra pax hominibus bonae voluntatis."

"Sarah," Dad said quietly. "We're Jewish."

"Sure, Dad," I whispered. "And Martin's an atheist. It's just a game."

Dad shrugged.

Martin went on. He'd memorized the mass, I guess.

And we stared out at the sea.

At last Martin came to an end. ". . . Agnus Dei, qui tollis peccata mundi, dona nobis pacem."

He was silent, then looked at us.

"Amen," we said.

The breeze was cool. I shivered a little.

After a long moment, Don spoke. "And so," he said, "you stand forlorn on the Severn shore, the sounds of the sea and the wind about you. The stars wheel overhead. But there is nothing more, no fantastical boat bearing . . ."

"Whoa," said Karen. "Look at that."

It was a shooting star, a big one. The streak stretched across half the sky. As it passed over the horizon, it seemed, briefly, as if there were a flash out there in the sea.

"Nice," said Don.

The sound of surf surrounded us. The breeze was cool. The chaotic, tossing waves broke into spray, and the foam caught the moon, throwing up glints of light. Out there, it was difficult to tell where sea ended and sky began. But the sky was peppered with stars, and the sea was dark. Dark, except that . . .

"There's a glow out there," I said.

"I see it," said Karen. "It's pretty faint."

"Isn't it where the meteor hit?" said Martin.

"It looks like the same direction," I said.

Rupert stood up and sniffed the breeze.

The air smelled salt. I was definitely shivering.

"Must be a ship's running lights," Dad said.

We watched a little longer.

"It's getting brighter," said Martin. "Maybe the ship is getting closer."

Rupert went into a point, nose extended toward the light, tail pointing backward. The only time I'd seen that before was when he smelled rabbit.

The surf crashed. The sky was dark enough, despite the lights of the Cape behind us, that you could easily distinguish the Milky Way. And out there shone the stars, immortal, impatient, uncaring, old beyond knowing and unfathomably distant. Silently, the noise of the ocean about us, we gazed south, out across the Atlantic.

The light got brighter.

"A . . . UFO?" asked Karen.

Martin snorted. "Come on, Karen," he said. "There's no such thing as . . ."

"It *is* a ship," I said. My eyes are better than average. I've never needed glasses. "But . . ."

Goosebumps ran down my arms.

"But we're not seeing running lights."

My dad squinted. "What, then?"

I didn't answer. In a few moments, they saw it too.

The entire ship was glowing: hull, superstructure, and deck—glowing a faint, ethereal green, the color of those glow-in-the-dark bracelets they sell at carnivals. It seemed to shimmer, as if it were there but not there.

"Looks military," said my dad. There were gun emplacements. But it was pretty small for a warship.

It came toward us.

"No such thing as . . . ghosts, Martin?" said Karen softly. Martin, slackjawed, made no answer.

It was larger now, perhaps a quarter mile offshore, bearing directly toward our point on the beach. We stood there as if rooted.

"That's a PT boat," said my dad in wonderment.

It hove to a hundred feet offshore. I think we all gasped. We'd only seen it head-on before. Before it turned, it had not been apparent that—the ship had no stern.

It was as if the ship had been sliced in two, and the aft half was gone. No, not sliced—brutally smashed in two. The hull plates were torn, ragged. This was a ship that had been badly mistreated.

This was a ship that could not possibly be afloat.

This was a ghost ship in truth.

And at its bow were painted letters and a number. My eyes were best: "PT—PT-109," I read.

That meant nothing to me, but it did to my dad—my dad, the naval history buff. He stared at me. "It went down in the Solomons," he whispered. "1943. A Japanese destroyer rammed it amidships."

A rope ladder came tumbling over the side of the ship. A moment later, a dinghy followed, lowered on ropes. And then, a single man clambered down the ladder and into the dinghy.

The dinghy glowed as ethereally as the ship, but the man—oh, the man glowed brilliantly, a silver light, a bright light, burning like an incandescent lamp. He stood in the dinghy's bow, stood erect, and the dinghy made toward us.

There was no noise, no motor sound. No one labored at oars. And yet, the dinghy arrowed toward us, bobbing in the surf, and the man stood at its helm, erect and proud.

We watched, silent, amazed, but unafraid.

Suddenly, José whooped. "Don!" he shouted. "You're wrong!"

"Huh?"

"Our prayers are answered!"

Don looked astounded. "But . . . that's no medieval ship," he said. "How can. . . ? Arthur. . . ?"

"We do not stand on the Severn shore," said José. "We stand on the Massachusetts shore!"

Martin looked at him as if he were mad.

"The martyred King returns," José babbled, "in his nation's hour of need."

My dad was nodding, but the rest of us failed to understand.

Until the dinghy gritted on the beach, and John F. Kennedy stepped into the surf, wetting the trousers of his suit.

Rupert ran toward him, barking joyously.

About the Authors

Greg Costikyan is a professional game designer with more than twenty commercially published games to his credit. He has also published short stories and a novel.

Anne E. Crompton has written many short stories and eleven novels while raising her family in a small Massachusetts town. Among her novels are *Queen of Swords* and *The Sorcerer.* She is also the author of the picture book *The Winter Wife.*

Debra Doyle lives in New Hampshire with her husband James D. Macdonald and their four children. A Ph.D. in literature who occasionally teaches college English courses, Dr. Doyle has had many short stories and novels published in association with her husband, including the six *Circle of Magic* books and *Knight's Wird.*

Kathleen Kudlinski has published biographies and historical novels for young readers. She lives with her husband, children, and many pets on the edge of a lake in Guilford, Connecticut, writes nature columns for the local newspaper, and sometimes helps out with the Girl Scouts.

Anne McCaffrey is the best-selling and prize-winning author of the *Pern* novels, as well as dozens of other books, stories, and poems. She lives in Ireland and raises horses.

James D. Macdonald is the other half of the Doyle writing team. He is the author (with his wife) of numerous novels and short stories, and on his own, dozens of newspaper and magazine articles and movie reviews. He is currently the sysop of the Science Fiction and Fantasy RoundTable on GEnie, an international computer bulletin board system.

Diana L. Paxson is the author of many short stories and novels, a number of which are about Arthurian themes, including the best-selling *The White Raven,* a novel about Tristan and Isolde. A writer of bardic poetry, Ms. Paxson plays and composes for the Celtic harp. She lives with her husband in Berkeley, California.

Lynne Pledger has been the director of a family resource institute, an editor of a newsletter, and has researched and developed demonstrations of women's work in the living history museum Old Sturbridge Village. She lives in central Massachusetts with her husband and two children.

Terry Pratchett, British author of the best-selling Discworld fantasy series for—as he puts it—"adults of all ages" as well as several best-selling children's books, lives in the county of Somerset in England with his family and "makes computers do things they weren't meant to do."

Nancy Springer is the author of over ten novels of mythic fantasy and science fiction for adults and young adults, as well as several horse novels for young readers. The mother of a middle-school-age daughter and a teenage son, she lives with her husband and children in Dallastown, Pennsylvania.

Adam Stemple is a musician and composer who has six books to his credit and many published songs. A member of a rock band, his instruments include guitar, piano, cello, and mountain dulcimer. He lives in Minneapolis, Minnesota.

Mark W. Tiedemann has been working in one branch of photography or another for almost twenty years. A graduate of the Clarion Workshop in science fiction writing, his stories have appeared in several magazines. He lives with his wife in South St. Louis, Missouri.

Jane Yolen is the prize-winning author of over 100 books, including two previous Arthurian books, the novel *The Dragon's Boy* and the collection of stories and poems *Merlin's Booke.* She is also the author of the Caldecott-winning picture book *Owl Moon.* She lives with her husband in a big Victorian farmhouse in Hatfield, Massachusetts, and often visits her three grown children who live in other states.